Colton's Terrible Wonderful Year

Vincent Traughber Meis

Spectrum Books

Contents

To D

One

I can pinpoint the day my life started getting strange, and by strange, I mean grown-up. My parents had just picked me up at the police station. It was the first time I had gotten in trouble with law enforcement and my dads (yes; I have two dads) were upset and, I suppose, embarrassed, and a bunch of other emotions. Let me just say, my dads are the coolest people on earth and probably don't deserve the hard time I sometimes give them when I do stupid things and say stupid things and they get mad, and I get mad back. I don't even want to think about all the times we ended up in tears because, you know, life is hard, and I really love them, and they really love me.

Those times the three of us ended up blubbering idiots were the worst but later turned out to be the best when we finished the evening on the couch eating ice cream and watching a movie that we all agreed was terrible and laughed and cuddled under a blanket because evenings are always cold in San Francisco, including in the summer. And, even if they weren't, I loved the warmth and comfort of being in a family that wasn't afraid to show affection.

But coming home from the police station was tough. I walked into the house in front of my dads and was headed for my room, my happy place, feeling like everything would be okay if I could get to my room and close the door on all the bad stuff. But before I was halfway down the hall, I heard my dad's raised voice. "Where are you going?" That's my dad, Augie, August actually, who I call Dad.

It was pretty obvious, but I said, "To my room."

And my other dad chimed in. "No, you're not." His name is Ruben, but I call him Papi. He was born in Los Angeles, though his parents are from Mexico.

"Why not?"

"Did you think that was the end of it?" said Dad. "You've lost your screen time for a week and you will come home directly from school until further notice."

"I said I was sorry." I think I actually groaned like I was the most unfortunate teenager in the world, which I knew was a long, long way from the truth.

"Sorry doesn't cut it. There have to be consequences." That was Dad with the dreaded c-word, a favorite with parents, teachers, and, I guess, adults in general.

Here's the deal. My two best friends, Fer and Josh, and I went downtown after school and ended up in the Target store. It's not something we do a lot because we often have basketball practice or Fer has to go home and take care of his younger sibs because both his parents work or Josh has to do something because whichever one of his divorced parents he's with on a particular day is on his case. And Dad is now home all the time because he took a leave of absence from his job at the Mission Branch of the public library so he could pursue writing full time. If I'm not home by a certain time, I get the third degree. But the way the stars lined up that day, we didn't have basketball practice. Fer's mom stayed home because the clients she cooks for were out of town; it was the part of the week Josh was with his dad and his dad was working late; and my dad went to some writing event in Berkeley and wouldn't be home until dinnertime. We were free. It was amazing how rarely that happened on a weekday.

We got on a BART train at 16th Street and got off at Powell Street, which is sort of the center of the universe when it comes to San Francisco. We laughed at the long line of tourists waiting to ride the cable car halfway to the stars, knowing that locals just walk up a block or two and hop on. And hitting up the tourists for a handout were representatives of the city's homeless population, who took advantage of the captive audience. There were the Jesus Saves people with placards telling everybody to repent (fat chance in San Francisco) and street musicians and performers also preying on the out-of-towners to make a buck. Along the railing looking over the station plaza, chess players hunched over makeshift tables, bundled in layers of clothing and wearing fingerless gloves. And because it was a workday there were all the dressed-up businesspeople who worked downtown, intermingling with the shoppers and tourists and people sporting every fashion statement you could imagine. There were plenty of people for us to gawk at.

We entertained ourselves by walking around that area

for a while, and then decided we were hungry and ended up at Super Duper, a burger place. We pooled our resources and found that burgers weren't in our budget, so we got two orders of fries that we shared and one soda with three straws. Fer started doing silly things with the fries, like sticking two of them in his nose, causing us to laugh hysterically. We played 'see food' and got dirty looks from the older couple at the next table. It was all pretty stupid, but the sense of feeling good with each other was real and made me appreciate how lucky I was to have great friends.

Josh said we should go over to Target to check out the latest video games like Jedi: Fallen Order or Outer Wilds. We found the cabinets where they keep the games and Josh's eyes got as big and shiny as the compact discs we so treasured. He whispered that they forgot to lock the cabinet. We looked around and saw the salesperson had a line of people at the register, but a security guard had his eye on us.

Josh put an arm around my shoulders and said, "Cole, why don't you take a walk a few aisles over to the... whatever... hardware section?"

"Why?"

He nodded his head slightly toward the guard. "To get him off our asses."

"Why me?"

Josh tilted his head down and looked out of the corner of his eyes. "Dude."

With one word and a sly look, no further communication was needed. Josh was white, blond, blue-eyed, the whole nine yards. Though Fer was Mexican, he wasn't so obvious, and I don't mean to sound racist. He was taller than most of the Mexican kids at school and had lighter skin because one of his grandparents was from Galicia, Spain. But me, I was Black. Half-Black to be precise. I had the kinky hair, medium dark skin, and facial features of the surrogate mom who had me for my dads.

Josh's plan worked like a charm. I walked toward the sports section and picked up a basketball. The guard stood at the end of the aisle and none too subtly watched me. I went to the automotive section and started looking at the cell phone holders. Yeah, like I had my own car at fourteen. There he was, down the aisle. I glanced at him, and he picked up a bottle of car wash, examining the label. Getting back to what made that day different, that day strange, was the racism. Sure, there had been other examples in my years on this planet, people making racist comments either deliberately or out of ignorance. But what happened in the Target store hit me up the side of my head and said, "Hey, man, you're Black and this is your life." I had this tingling feeling going up and down my spine and my face felt hot. There were three of us in a public situation, but I was the one they followed, and Josh recognized it as a given. "Fuck it," I mumbled and walked two aisles down, drawing the security guard further away from my friends like my skin was a magnet.

I learned later that Josh had kneeled like he was tying his shoe and Fer stood, blocking him from view. He slid the glass door open, grabbed a couple of discs, and stuck them under his shirt, tucking them into his pants. He stood up and said, "I have to take a whiz. Go find Cole and come to the restroom." Of course, we had to remove the AF security stickers from the packaging. We all met up in the bathroom and Josh went in a stall. We hadn't talked about doing this, so it was a bit weird that Josh had a razor blade with him to cut out the stickers. We were all buzzed with the notion we were committing a crime and were going to get away with it. I was still nervous as hell, though.

When we left the restroom, the security guard was right there with his arms crossed. We froze. He was a big guy with a shiny white dome and a belly for days. We probably could have scattered and outrun him, but he anticipated that. "We've got all your faces on camera, so don't even think about running."

They took us to Mission Police Station and called our parents. Papi came from work and Dad left the writing event early. Josh's dad was furious when he came and saw us sitting on a bench. He looked directly at me like it was all my fault. Each of the parents met with the police. Since none of us had any previous offenses and we were on the basketball team, blah, blah, blah, we just got a warning and a lecture.

When we got home, I was a mess because it had been scary, and I hated disappointing my dads. It also gave them fuel for criticizing my friends, who they weren't pleased with, anyway. Fer and Josh were polite enough when they came over to the house, but sometimes we would go into my room and play video games and start yelling and screaming. My parents hated that. And then there were the texts messages they had read when they put some kind of software on my phone. There was some sex stuff and bad language, pretty normal four-teen-year-old things. That led to them confiscating my phone for two weeks. So, Fer and Josh were already on my dads' shitlist. And now this. Things were tense on all sides. But through it all was that one thing that really got to me, the racism.

I shuffled back down the hallway into the living room and almost had to laugh at Dad's surprised expression that he still held the power of a parent. Neither of my dads were the type that enjoyed discipline. Josh told me that his father seemed to get off on punishing him, es-pecially when he was little, and he used to spank him. My dads never laid a finger on me though the truth is the psychological stuff was so bad, I sometimes wished they would just spank me and get it over with.

Dad and Papi sat on the sofa, and I slouched in an armchair, arms crossed, my butt nearly off the edge, and my long legs extended halfway across the room. I stared at my feet, which looked gigantic, too big for my scrawny legs. I couldn't wait until I started growing out instead of just up. Papi said I was like a wad of bubble gum that got stretched out to the limit. From where I was sitting, I could see pictures of me as a chubby baby on the mantel. And then one day that fat disappeared. "Don't worry," said Papi, "it'll come back when you least expect it and don't want it."

I could tell Dad held himself back from scolding me to sit up straight. One thing at a time. "Why would you steal something rather than use your savings to pay for it or ask us to buy it for your birthday?"

I avoided the issue that technically it hadn't been me who stole the games. I didn't want to rat out Josh. "You don't know what it's like being Black in a store, having them follow you around, looking at you funny. But I bet my mom knows."

My dads looked like I had just punched them in the stomach and turned to each other, not sure how to respond. We'd had the discussion where they admitted neither of them knew exactly what it was like to be Black, though they both knew something of prejudice. Dad, being Jewish and gay, even growing up in the Bay Area, had suffered taunts at school and being called Jew faggot. And Papi was often lumped in with drug runners and gang members, not to mention all the other insulting names people called Mexicans. I know they agonized over not really knowing how to have the conversation that Black parents had with their kids to keep them alive.

They had told me about Joy, the surrogate mother I had never met, and I had expressed on a number of occasions that I wanted to meet her. Dad and Papi had argued in recent months about it. In the process of bringing me into the world, Augie, Ruben, and Joy had agreed that she would take no part in my life. But, with time, Papi had softened his position, believing Joy deserved the opportunity to accept or reject knowing her son. Not that she would participate or have any responsibilities. Only to know. Dad had his angry face on, not happy Papi had changed his position.

Joy was back in Los Angeles, singing with a band, but she was unsure about meeting me. It seems Papi had contacted her, and I had overheard a heated discussion about it. Of course, I wanted to meet her because she was the one who gave birth to me and shared my skin color, but the fact that she was a singer blew my mind. I spent hours listening to music and had this fantasy that one day I would be sitting around with my friends, and we would hear her on a mixtape or YouTube and I'd say, "That's my mom."

"I admit Joy would know better than we do what you must deal with in public," said Papi. "And there's a good chance you'll be able to talk to her about it someday." Dad tensed at his husband's words.

"You always say that. But when?"

"I don't know, Colie."

"Have you talked to her about meeting?"

Dad heaved a sigh. "Go ahead. You might as well tell him."

I sat up, put my hands on my knees, and opened my eyes wide. "Tell me what?"

"I talked to her a couple of weeks ago," said Papi. "I asked if she was open to a meeting. She's not sure about, you know, meeting you. It's been so long."

"We can't force it, Cole," said Dad. "If she doesn't want to, she doesn't want to."

"She didn't say she didn't want to. She said she's not sure." My voice came out loud and a little squeakier than I would have liked. I try to be respectful, but sometimes it's hard to control myself and my voice takes off. "It's not the same. You should let me talk to her."

"Relax, mijo. You know we love you more than any-thing, right?" said Papi. That was kind of out of left field. If there's a good cop/bad cop situation with my dads, Papi was usually the good one.

I fell back into my slouch position. "Yeah. But I don't understand why it's such a big deal for me to meet my mother."

Dad perked up like he had a brainstorm. "I've been thinking of something and now seems the perfect time to give it life. We need a family vacation."

I sat up again. "To LA?"

"Oh, brother," said Dad. "You're determined. I'll give you that. But no. Not LA. Someplace far away. I was think-ing... Thailand? I always wanted to go there. We could go during your winter break, and, Ruben, you said you had some vacation time you have to use before the end of the year."

We both looked at Dad like he had gone mental.

Papi was always more rational and in charge of the household budget. He shook his head. "We can't afford it."

"Don't worry about it. I've got this. I still have money from the sale of Mom's house," said Dad.

"What's in Thailand?" I asked. "That sounds boring. Do they have Internet and stuff?"

"They have everything. It's a modern country. Great beaches, beautiful temples, and the food is super."

"Really, Dad," I said with an exaggerated eye roll. I mean beaches are cool, but I would take a hard pass on temples. And the food? There were tons of Thai restaurants all over town. We didn't need to go thousands of miles to eat it.

"I don't know," said Papi. "It's so far. And you didn't even talk to me about this. You just throw it out there. We're supposed to talk about things."

Dad glared at both of us like he couldn't comprehend why we were being hard-headed nincompoops. "We're talking now!" Since he left his stable job as a librarian to pursue writing, he'd been a little more intense lately. He was writing a novel, but he wouldn't tell us what it was about. I also knew he was worried about my entering the danger zone of a Black teenager. He and Papi had been arguing more than usual, maybe feeling the strain rather than the joy of being together for so many years, like seventeen or something. And now I wanted to bring the surrogate mom back into their lives with all its uncertainties. I suppose for him, getting as far away as possible from all that seemed a perfect idea.

"Come on, Augie," said Papi. "Don't be angry."

Dad ignored his husband and turned to me. "They also have a lot of elephants in Thailand."

"Elephants?" My interest kicked up a notch. As a kid, I had always loved stories about elephants. My favorite book when I was three was The Saggy Baggy Elephant. I requested they read it to me every night. I had elephant stuffed animals and an elephant piggy bank, though when Josh and Her started coming over, I had hid them in the closet.

A bit of joy, or maybe it was just desperation, came

into Dad's eyes. "You can go to preserves and spend the day taking care of them. You can get up close and touch them."

That actually sounded cool. "I'd like that."

"I don't know," said Papi. "You mean spend Christmas and New Year's away?"

"It would be great," said Dad. "We've never done a trip like that as a family."

My expression turned sour again. "I see what you're doing. We're supposed to be talking about my mom."

"I promise as soon as we get back, we'll plan a weekend in Los Angeles," said Dad. "We'll tell Joy we're coming to town whether she wants to meet or not. It will force her hand."

"Okay. You promised. I'm going to hold you to it."

And this is a perfect example of how much my dads hated being disciplinarians. We had begun with the very tense and humiliating situation where I had been picked up for shoplifting, and we ended up talking about a trip to Thailand. The year following that conversation only got weirder. And I couldn't get rid of that bug of racism buzzing around in my brain. When I was finally released from the living room torture chamber and able to go to my room, I really wanted to talk to Fer and Josh about what had happened at Target, but my dads had confis-cated my phone again.

Two

Next thing I knew I was waking up to this weird-ass bird call, kowell, kowell and hearing waves hitting the beach. It was early and I could see pink sky through the sheer curtains. And then it hit me. We were like a million miles from home, and I didn't know what day it was. I was a little sweaty because my dads didn't want the air conditioning on so we could have the windows open and hear the sounds of the waves. I got up from my bed in the sleeping alcove of our room, and in walking toward the bathroom, I saw Papi still asleep, but Dad wasn't in bed. He wasn't in the bathroom either. I had this sudden panicky feeling, and I didn't know why. We were at a posh resort on an island, not in a high-crime district of a big city like Bangkok. When we had finalized the trip to Thailand, we watched this martial arts movie, The Protector, where Tony Jaa battles an evil crime syndicate that stole two elephants (Oh, no!). The action scenes were amazing, but Bangkok looked like a pretty scary place.

I got dressed, pulling board shorts over the boxers I slept in and throwing a tank top over my head, loving that vacay wear was all you needed day or night in this place. I quietly opened the door so as not to wake Papi and slipped out just as that bird, or whatever it was, revved up its kowell, kowell again. Damn, it was loud and kind of creepy. It made me feel like we were on a faraway planet, humid and smelling of exotic flowers and a sour, salty odor from the sea. I expected Tony Jaa from the movie to pop out from behind a bird of paradise and start doing his moves.

Despite the early hour, the place was busy with re-sort workers running around, making everything perfect. Women in long skirts of Thai silk filled the basins at each doorstep with fresh water and arranged hibiscus, orchid, and some other kind of flowers to float on the surface. A gourd was placed next to the basins so we could rinse off our sandy feet with perfumed water when we came back from the beach. How classy is that? I walked over to the pool area where the attendant rolled up red towels and assembled them in a large basket to look like petals of a rose. He smiled at me. Thailand, 'The Land of Smiles' as we had seen on billboards everywhere since we arrived. I sometimes wondered if those smiles were real or they were like those waiters at home who come to the table, "Hi, my name is Josie..." hoping for a big tip. I shouldn't be negative. My dads are always telling me that.

On the other side of the pool, silent restaurant work-ers darted back and forth in the open-air dining room, preparing the breakfast buffet. I thought maybe Dad had gone for a coffee, but I didn't see him in the restaurant.

I retraced my steps along the path with accent lights on either side, trying not to make too much noise in my flip-flops as there was a peaceful silence all around, like being in a library or church. A whole bunch of strange plants gave off this tropical vibe, and I recognized the smell of jasmine because we had a bush in the yard at home. Red lanterns hung from the trees like I was in an Asian garden, which, come to think of it, I was. Yes, we were in Asia, thousands of miles from home. It didn't feel real yet. I heard the bird again, loud and very close, but I couldn't see it. And then the woman, who had checked us in, padded toward me along the path, hugging a clipboard to her chest. She smiled, bowed slightly and said, "Sawatdee kaa."

Dad had told me the correct response was Sawatdee krap, but I couldn't say the 'crap' part with a straight face. I didn't want to disrespect anybody's language. It just sounded weird. I smiled and made an awkward bow back to her. I knew she spoke English, so I asked, "Could you tell me what that bird is?"

"Oh, this is Asian koel. Male singing for husband... I mean, wife." She giggled at her mistake and put one hand over her mouth. "Always in the morning. Hope it not wake you."

"No, no. It's the jetlag, mostly."

I was about to ask her if she had seen my dad, but at the same moment, I caught sight of him out near the water on a giant flat rock between two small beaches. He stood near the edge where the waves crashed, leaning like he might jump into the water. "Oh, there's my dad," I said and bowed again, leaving her smiling and bowing.

I approached from behind, and he must have heard my flip-flops because he spun around with a wild look in his eyes. "Hi, Dad. Did I scare you?"

He gave his crooked dad smile and unclenched his fists. "No. Only surprised. What are you doing up?"

"That bird woke me up. A koel or something."

"And Papi?"

"He's still sleeping."

"How are you doing with the time change?"

"It's weird, right? It's still yesterday at home."

We sat on a wooden bench a little damp with morning dew, looking out on the Gulf of Thailand under a partially overcast sky. Across the bay, lights twinkled while the rosy horizon changed to pink.

"This place is really cool," I said.

"You like it? I thought you might." I leaned toward my father, and he wrapped his arm around me.

"I'm sorry if I've been a problem lately."

"Being your age isn't easy, everything changing. And I guess having two dads makes it more complicated."

"Not that much. Only if you break up."

"Why would you say that?"

"I hear you and Papi fighting sometimes. It would be my fault."

"Oh, no, honey. If Papi and I ever separate, it won't be because of you."

I tensed. "You mean there's a chance it might happen?"

"Not even close. What I mean to say is there are very few things in life that are certain and forever, except for our love for you, of course. Couples have disagreements. It's normal."

I settled back into the crook of his arm, satisfied, relaxed. "Do they have elephants on this island?"

He laughed. "I don't think so. We'll have to wait until Chiang Mai."

It felt nice and relaxed to be there with my dad, but sometimes stupid things pop into my head even when I think I've brushed them aside, at least, for the time being.

"Why do you think he did it?" I said in a dreamy voice.

"Who? What?"

"Josh."

He let out a big sigh. "I don't know, Cole. I'm guessing his father put pressure on him."

"You believe me, right? The whole thing wasn't my idea."

"Of course, I do."

The incident at Target had been on a Friday. Since I didn't have my cell phone and we didn't have a landline, I went by Josh's place on Saturday. His parents had bought one of those new condos on Harrison Street a few blocks from our house. His mom still lived there after they split up. I buzzed their apartment on the intercom and his mom answered. "Hi, this is Colton. Is Josh there?"

There was a moment of silence. "No, he's at his dad's."

"Oh, okay. Sorry to bother you."

"No problem." And she clicked off. That was doubly weird. For one thing, I knew it was his weekend to be with his mom. And secondly, she, normally very friendly with me, had rudely cut me off. I had a sinking feeling in my stomach. I went over to Fer's who lived on Folsom. He came to the door but said he couldn't come out because he was grounded.

"Have you talked to Josh?"

"Nah, man." His father came up behind him and his shoulders tensed. "I'll see you at school on Monday."

I didn't see Fer or Josh until basketball practice after school. Everything seemed pretty normal until we got in the locker room after practice. Josh rushed into the showers and got dressed quickly. Strange behavior for him, who was Mr. Sociable and loved to joke around.

As he was out the door, I shouted, "Hey, Josh. Wait up."

"Can't. My dad's picking me up. See ya."

I looked at Fer. "What's going on?"

He shrugged his shoulders. "Don't worry about it."

"Is he ghosting me?"

"No way. I think his dad came down hard on him."

Josh continued to avoid me. I saw him in the hall one day and asked him what was going on. "Nothing," he said. "I've got to get my grades up or there will be hell to pay."

Josh, Fer, and I had been best friends for years. We got really close in middle school when we played on the basketball team. They were like the brothers I'd never had. Josh once punched this guy for calling me a nigger. We had each other's backs. We played hours of video games and talked about girls we liked. Fer and I went camping a couple of times with Josh's family in Lake Tahoe. We'd never had fights, just the usual teasing with two of the three ganging up on the third.

A few days after Josh's ghosting/not ghosting, Fer and I were walking home, and I made him spill the beans. "Fer, you gotta tell me what's going on with Josh. He's being hella weird. You know something."

It took a while, but I finally got it out of him. Josh's dad threatened him with boarding school and being grounded for the rest of the year and all kinds of stuff. Fer said Josh was so freaked that he told his dad that ripping off the video games had been my idea, and I had even come up with the plan to distract the security guard, knowing he would follow me because I was Black.

I was stunned. "That is so screwed up!"

"Yeah, but it will all blow over. Don't worry about it."

I always had this impression that Fer's loyalties lay more with Josh than with me. I stopped walking and took his arm. "Are you taking his side?"

He wrenched his arm out of my grip. "Chill, man. You're acting like he broke up with you or something."

"Fuck you, Fer."

Everybody always used to say how cool it was that a Black guy, a white guy, and a Latino were best friends. We didn't even think about it. Best friends don't see color, right? But when push came to shove, they threw me under the bus. I was desperate to ask Fer if he told Josh how screwed up it was to say it was all my idea. I was dying to know if he stood up for me, but I was afraid of the answer. I walked away.

On the other side of the world, I still felt the pain, sitting on the bench in Thailand with my dad, and I was happy to be so far away from my traitorous friends. I don't know if it was jetlag or being in my father's arms or what, but I began to cry. He pulled me closer. What I said about Dad being the bad cop wasn't fair. Oh, sure, his face could go all hard and twitchy, like it was the end of the world because I forgot to brush my teeth, but I knew he did it for my own good. He held me and let me cry and I loved him so much at that moment I could have burst. After a few minutes of sobbing, my breathing slowed, and a few minutes later I was asleep snuggled against him with his arm around me.

Three

We were the first ones at the breakfast buffet with everything you could imagine, including both Western and Thai food, hot and cold, tables filled with carved fruit and tropical juices, pastries and cereals, soups and hot dishes. I had never seen anything like it. The staff, all dressed in matching uniforms, the women in long black skirts and red blouses and the men in red tunics and black pants, hovered ready to meet our every need.

Soon after we sat down with our first plates of food, another family arrived, an interracial couple who looked to be about the same age as my parents, early to mid-forties, white father, Black mother, two children: a young man around twenty and a girl close to my age. Despite the open-air restaurant being quite large, they took the table right next to ours and greeted us with "Good Morning." Dad made a comment about the British accent and raised his eyebrows at Papi. I was so focused on my pancakes, I didn't take much notice.

On the juice table was a do-it-yourself juicer next to a large tray of cut-up fruit and vegetables. I had made a beet, ginger, carrot, apple juice. It was the color of blood.

When I went back for seconds, this time pastries and fruit, I noticed the girl was struggling with the juicer. I put my plate down and went to help her. That was when I first noticed how pretty she was, and I could feel my heartbeat ramp up. I told her I could make her the best juice ever, and she burst into laughter. Her laugh made me feel all fuzzy inside and her brown eyes sparkled.

At school there were a few girls I liked, but I had never felt anything for a girl with the same skin color as me. I looked over at my dads and saw Dad tap Papi's arm and nose-point at us just because I was having a little friendly exchange with a girl. Out of the corner of my eye, I saw the girl's mother look over at Dad and Papi with a smile. Parents are so weird sometimes. What was the big deal?

The brother turned around and motioned to his sister. "Could you make me one too? That is, if you're not too busy." She pretended not to hear him.

"What kind would you like?" I said to him.

"How about apple carrot?"

"You got it."

"You don't have to," said the girl. She shook her head as if disgusted her brother always had to butt into her affairs.

I began filling the juicer with carrot and apple pieces. "What's your name?"

"Olivia," she said.

"I'm Colton, but most people call me Cole."

"My parents call me Livie, but I prefer Olivia."

I finished the juice and started toward the table to give it to her brother. Olivia had this bewildered look on her face like I had asked her to dance and then walked away.

"That's lovely. Thank you," said the brother. "My name's Devlin." The first thing I noticed about Devlin was his eyes, a blue-gray color, the kind of thing that makes you do a double take. His skin was dark like mine and he had the kinky hair, so he was definitely Black. I had never noticed a Black guy with such light eyes.

"I'm Cole. Those are my dads over there." Everyone smiled except the father, who knitted his eyebrows. The father was pasty white with blond hair and, surprise, blue-gray eyes.

I went back to Olivia and immediately looked at her eye color, a very soft brown. As soon as I was by her side, I swear her head lifted, and her spirit seemed to fly. I suppose I could have exaggerated my effect. We spent a few more minutes talking about I don't know what and then returned to our respective tables.

As I sat down with a full plate, Papi wouldn't let up with his enthusiasm. "What's her name?"

"Olivia." I tried to show no excitement whatsoever.

"You guys were talking a lot," Papi continued.

"She needed help with the juicer. That's all." I took a large bite of a Danish, and the dark fuzz on my upper lip became smeared with jam. I licked it off before Olivia could look over and see berry stuck to my emerging mustache. I stared at the pastry as if it was a lot more fascinating than talking to my parents about any feelings related to meeting a girl.

A few months back, I had that talk with my dads about the possibility of my being gay and how they would love me no matter which way things turned out. It seemed unnecessary and a little awkward because I just knew in my gut they felt that way. "I like girls," I said. "Sorry." I meant it like a joke. Dad nodded like he expected as much, but Papi's face totally unwrinkled with relief, like he had just taken a very satisfying dump, and then he got all serious.

"We certainly didn't expect you to be gay because we are," said Papi.

"I know. But, while we're on the subject, why do you think you guys are gay?"

Since I was little, they had given me the simplified version: some boys like girls, and some boys like other boys, and some girls like other girls. In recent years they had added: some boys feel like they're really a girl inside and some girls feel they're boys trapped in a girl's body. But I felt I was old enough for the not-so-simplified version.

Papi started with, "I don't think it's time..."

Dad cut him off. "If he's asking, he's old enough."

I sensed they weren't exactly on the same page about discussing homosexuality or what caused it. "Yeah, you're right," said Papi.

"Homosexuality has been a topic of discussion probably as long as humans have been discussing," said Dad. "By the way, there are multiple examples of same-sex activity in the animal kingdom, so don't think it's just humans. Basically, the theories fall into two camps, nature versus nurture."

"What does that mean?" I asked.

"It used to be popular to think it was something that

happened in the way someone was raised or something in the environment of a person growing up. That's nurture. Things like a mother was overbearing, or a father was distant. In recent years, with the advancement of scientific experiments and studies, people started leaning toward nature or Lady Gaga's 'born this way' argument."

"What's Lady Gaga have to do with it?" I asked.

"Her song 'Born this Way' was adopted by the gay community as an anthem that expresses the idea we were born gay. You were still a baby when it came out and you used to dance around the house singing 'born this way.'"

"I do not remember that. But there goes the nurture theory. That song should have made me gay."

Both my dads laughed. "Truth be told," said Papi, "the song wasn't just about being gay. It was about empowering all kinds of minorities and people who don't fit into norms."

"So, of course, they had to do a million research studies to pinpoint the chromosome or the hormone or neuron or some biological explanation why people exhibited attraction to people of the same sex," said Dad.

"Did they find it?" I asked.

Dad got all huffy. "No. And I'm glad they didn't. It's got to be more complicated than a single genetic diversion from the norm. If they definitively find something, humans being the way they are, will want to 'fix it,'" (he totally used air quotes for that), "and I don't think it's anything that should be fixed. I love being gay. I love the fact that I found and married Papi, and we were able to have you. Imagine how boring the world would be without homosexuals, without Michelangelo and Oscar Wilde and E. M. Forster and Lorraine Hansberry and Frida Khalo and Walt Whitman."

I didn't know who half those people were, but when Dad got on a roll, you couldn't help but be swept up in it. Papi, who'd had a pretty serious expression on his face throughout the discussion, was now smiling and he high-fived his husband.

"That's cool and all, but I'm still not sure why you guys are gay."

"Why does there have to be a reason? The point is, we should accept everybody the way they are, like we accept left-handed people and people who fart a lot."

"Oh, God, Dad! Really?"

Four

After breakfast, Dad suggested visiting a temple we could walk to no more than two hundred yards up the road. "It looks pretty cool in the pictures. It's called Wat Rachathammaram, which means Snake Stone Temple."

"Can I stay here?" I said. "I kinda want to go in the pool."

They gave me a sly look, like they knew exactly why I wanted to go straight to the pool. I was anxious to continue my conversation with Olivia and I didn't know how long they were staying at the resort. What if they were leaving that day?

"You can spend all afternoon at the pool," said Dad. "This trip is about doing cultural stuff as well as having fun. As a family."

I looked at Papi for support. "Dad's right," said Papi. "I think every day we should try to do something cultural in the morning, have lunch, and then play in the afternoon."

"But a temple?"

"Open mind, remember? We're going to see lots of new things. Some of it you'll like and some not. But we must stay open to new experiences. We have swimming pools back home."

The sight of the reddish spires of the temple rising against a blue, blue sky drew a "Wow" even from me. The large gates were open, but the complex was empty. "This is great," said Dad. "We can roam the grounds comfortably with no crowds and the heat of the day still a couple of hours away."

We took off our shoes to enter the temple and felt the cool, polished red marble under our feet. The walls and ceiling were covered with bas-relief images of gods in quiet poses and others in chaos, eating the sun or riding on wild boars. Sea demons emerged from stormy waves and a huge fish swallowed a person while ape warriors fought in the name of their god. I had to admit the images were rad, like I was looking at a comic book. Instead of having dialogue bubbles to follow the stories, there were explication panels, which they were nice enough to put in English as well as Thai. I took pictures because I wanted to show them to a friend at school who liked to draw weird stuff.

Everything inside the temple was red clay except the golden Buddha sitting on a pedestal guarded by two gray elephants on either side.

"I was wrong," said Dad. "There are elephants on Koh Samui."

"Ha ha," I said. "I want to see real elephants. You promised."

Outside in the courtyard, a large Buddha sat under a huge bodhi tree, surrounded by funny little statues of royalty and roosters.

I leaned toward the Buddha and scrunched my eyes.

"The Buddha has a black face. Was he Black?"

"He was Indian, so he wasn't exactly white," said Papi. "He's not usually represented with such dark skin. Mr. Librarian?"

"It's Mr. Writer now," Dad said with a chuckle.

Papi and I looked at each other and smirked. "Sorry. We forgot." Dad has a reputation for being mister know-it-all. He does manage to hold a ton of information in his head from the hundreds of books he's read. I admire him for that, but there are times he's a little over the top.

"I'm sure you will both be very surprised I don't have an answer. We're going to see lots of Buddhas, so we have to keep our eyes open for another black one."

Beyond the tree was a tall structure with a golden dome topped with a pointy steeple. "What is that for?" I asked.

"That one I can answer. It's called a stupa. They hold the relics of holy men. This one must have been super important. Over there are a bunch of smaller stupas for the lesser guys."

Behind the large stupa, we descended a double-wide stairway with brightly painted giant serpents running down either side, leading to huge red and gold cobra heads rising from the posts at the bottom. Tied around the necks of the cobras were multi-colored ribbons and garlands of marigold flowers. Offered for good luck, Dad explained. The beach at the foot of the steps was deserted and littered with plastic bottles and bags. "Can I go in the water?" I asked.

"The beach is nicer back at the resort," said Papi. "Let's

go have some lunch."

I spent the whole lunch worried because the British family was nowhere in sight. They had probably checked out, and I had missed one more opportunity to talk to Olivia thanks to our visit to that stupid temple.

With full bellies and the afternoon heating up, we lined up in lounge chairs next to the pool but facing out to sea. The pool attendant rushed over with fresh towels. A short time later, when I was almost asleep in my chair, I heard this faint giggle, and I whipped my head around to see the British family arriving. Thank you, Buddha. I didn't grow up with any kind of religion, but I had prayed to that black Buddha at the temple in hopes I would see her again. Everybody said hi, and they occupied the next four chairs in the row. The parents, Nigel and Joanna Saxton, introduced themselves, and Dad told them about the temple we had visited. Unfortunately, Olivia ended up farthest from me in the last chair of the row.

"What are you reading?" Dad asked Nigel.

Nigel held up Trevor Noah's Born a Crime. "Appalling! The stories of apartheid. And yet, he tells it in such an entertaining way."

Dad spouted off everything he knew about the book and Trevor Noah, in general. Nigel rested the book on his chest. "And to what do you dedicate your life if you don't mind me asking?"

"I'm a librarian, but I've taken a leave to write. Got a little inheritance from my mom."

"Splendid. What kind of things do you write? The great American novel perhaps?"

"My ambitions aren't so lofty. I'm working on a Young Adult novel, trying to make sense of what my son is going through."

Really, Dad? Good luck with that. I kept glancing at Olivia. She was stretched out in a red checkered swimsuit and she looked beautiful, like a model with long brown legs.

"If you could make sense of it, that would be a lofty achievement," said Nigel. "The teenage years are endlessly challenging."

Uh... try being a Black teenager and you'll see how challenging.

"It's about two boys. One doesn't have a mother and longs for one to match his skin color. The other has a mother who perfectly matches his skin, but he doesn't want her because he's angry."

This was annoying. I never heard him talk about the book before. I can hear you, Dad. Are you writing about me?

"Ah, yes. Boys and their mothers," said Nigel.

"I haven't turned out so bad, have I?" said Devlin.

"Not too bad, poppet." Nigel chuckled. "Now, if you could just get a proper job."

"Just wait until I leave home. You'll be crying for me to come back."

"That'll be the day."

"Stop, you two," said Joanna. "What are our friends to think?"

"Yes, lovey." Nigel wiped his forehead and stood up. "I'm not used to this heat. Excuse me. I'm going for a swim."

Devlin slid over to the chair next to Dad after Nigel made his way down to the beach. He was equally chatty, asking lots of questions about where we lived and what we had seen on the trip so far. Devlin was as handsome as his sister was beautiful. His hair was shaved close on the sides and he'd let it grow long on top and had a sort of two strand twist style. He was tall and in great shape, making me think I needed to start working out if I was going to look as good as him by the time I was twenty.

It was funny to hear a British accent coming from a Black guy. "Look at that, mate," said Devlin. I opened one eye to see what he was talking about.

Devlin pointed out a black butterfly that had landed on a nearby bush. It fanned its wings, and then took off into the air, dancing around us before finally landing on Dad's knee. Its wings were iridescent with little dots of yellow. "I feel special," whispered Dad.

"And no doubt you are," said Devlin. "Make a wish!"

Papi looked up from his book and chuckled softly.

Okay, I'd had about enough. I hadn't been able to catch Olivia once looking over at me. It seemed to be getting hotter every minute. The temperature, I mean. I jumped up and dove in the pool. I swam around and then did a whole length of the pool underwater. When I came up, there was Olivia, sitting on the edge and dangling her feet in the water. She obviously wanted to talk to me, right? Very cool-like, I made my way over to her.

"Hi, Olivia."

"How's the water?"

"It's great. But it could be better."

"What do you mean?"

"If you were in it." Oh, my God. What was I doing? Did I really say that?

She looked surprised at first and then laughed as she dropped into the water. I backed up and threw a small rubber ball I had found floating in the water. It landed near her and splashed water on her face. "Hey!" She looked angry, and I thought I had screwed up.

"Sorry."

She threw the ball back hard, and it hit me right in my forehead. It didn't hurt, but I covered my face with my hand as if it did. She swam over close to me. "Are you alright?"

"I'll live." I laughed and dove for the ball that floated on the surface nearby. I came up and faked like I was going to throw the ball hard at her. She squealed and everyone turned to look at us. I tossed the ball softly, making it land a few feet from her. This time she dove under and came up holding the ball. Her long curly hair was now plastered to her back like thick ropes. We threw the ball back and forth a few times and then went over to the side of the pool, resting our arms on the hot tile and kicking our legs.

"How old are you?" I asked.

"I'm fifteen. And you?"

Since I was tall for my age, I could have lied and said I was fifteen, too. But I didn't want to start our... whatever with a lie. "I'm fourteen."

"You look older."

I loved her already. "Thanks." A couple of times I had

caught Papi craning his neck to see what we were doing. "Hey. Do you want to go swimming in the sea?"

"Absolutely. I suppose we should ask our parents."

Olivia and I stood over the adults and suppressed our giggles. Nigel had returned from the water and Papi had stopped his rubbernecking. They all seemed to be dozing. Dad was snoring. We could have slipped away to the sea or ridden off into the sunset on our imaginary horses.

I cleared my throat. "Olivia and I are going swimming in the sea."

Papi perked up first. "Okay. Wait. Are there sharks in the gulf?"

Devlin smiled. "There bloody well are, but attacks are rare. The guy at the bar told me there's never been an attack in this bay. I'll go in the water with them if you like."

"That would be sweet of you," said Dad. "Don't go out too far, Colton."

"I'm a good swimmer and so is Olivia."

Devlin jumped up. "I could use a dip. Tickety-boo!"

"You kids have a good time," said Nigel.

"Ruben, Augie, would you like to join us?" said Devlin.

"Bloody hell," Olivia mumbled under her breath.

So much for our alone time in the water. Devlin led us all down the path to the beach, and I got a good view of the large tattoo on the upper part of his back. "Your tattoo is awesome! What does it mean?" I asked him.

"It's a sak yant tattoo. I got it last year when I was in Thailand. It's called the paed tidt or eight directional yant that pulls in luck from all directions. It protects me while traveling."

"Cool," I said.

Olivia rolled her eyes.

"Can I get a tattoo, Papi?" said Dad in a silly voice.

"I'm sure it would look fabulous on your hairy back," said Papi.

"You had to ruin it for me, didn't you?"

At first, I was worried that Dad might be angry, but I was probably being overly sensitive to the recent tension between them. I really needed them to be okay. Everything else was going great, well, everything meaning Olivia. I was ignoring what was going on with my friends back home far, far away in a distant land.

Five

The bad news was that Olivia and I only had one more day together on the island. The following morning, both families would check out of the resort and go our separate ways, we to Chiang Mai and the Saxtons to Bangkok. Crushing! The good news was that we would all meet up again in Chiang Mai in about five days, five long days, and spend New Year's there. Awesome! In any case, I planned to make the most of our last day on Koh Samui. We still hadn't kissed since, like every waking moment, there were other family members breathing down our necks. Our two families had become inseparable. Olivia's parents and my dads had hit it off and spent hours drinking wine and talking about books, culture, and politics.

While the parents gabbed away, or 'chin wagged' as Olivia called it, we would sit nearby, talking about and listening to music, one ear bud in her ear and one in mine. I played some Clairo and Khai Dreams for her. She really liked Khai Dreams but was lukewarm on Clairo. Then I brought up a Beabadoobee song I had on my phone. She laughed. "You know she's British, grew up in West London, not far from me." Her accent was killing me. I could listen to it all day. I imagined introducing her to Fer and

Josh and seeing them freak out, first at her beauty, and then go mental when she opened her mouth with that accent. In the next moment, I remembered I was on the outs with Fer and Josh. It's funny how they automatically came up as the people I would like to introduce Olivia to. It left me a little depressed for two seconds. I glanced at Olivia's profile and my happiness was restored.

"Wow. West London. I didn't know that. What other artists are people listening to over there?"

She played a few songs by Grace Carter, Ama Lou, and Mabel, all incredible young Black British singers. I was blown away. Yeah. Young Black British female singers, and non-singers, my new thing. And then she played this amazing mellow hip-hop Easy Life song, "Sangria," featuring Arlo Parks, and I was on the floor. We played that song over and over. Olivia whispered, "Mum and Dad don't like it because the lyrics are a bit saucy." It became our song, and every time they got to the line, "I fucking hate it when you leave," we would mouth the words, bobbing our heads, smiling. Her music was a lot cooler than mine.

"Do you like Troye Sivan?" she asked.

"He's got a great voice, but he's so gay."

She jerked her head back so fast it popped the bud out of my ear, staring at me like I was crazy. She lifted her hand palm up in the direction of my dads.

"Who's so gay?" said Papi. What? Was he listening to every word?

"Troye Sivan. But I didn't mean it like that."

"What did you mean?" said Dad in a serious voice.

"It's just... nothing, really."

Papi came to my rescue. "I love his voice," he said.

"Me, too," said Devlin. Dad looked confused.

"Wait. You know who he is?" I said.

"Of course," said Papi. "I'm not that old. I keep up."

When it came to groupings, Devlin was often left in the middle, most of the time joining in the adult discussions, but would sometimes hang with us for swimming and water activities. He also told us about music he thought we should be listening to. "You guys should check out Nilüfer Yanya. She's from London, but she has Turkish, Irish and Barbadian roots. She has a lovely deep, husky voice."

"Whatever," said Olivia.

Even though Olivia was resistant to anything Dev might suggest, I made a mental note of the artist and planned to check her out.

There were times that Olivia and Dev seemed to enjoy doing things together despite their going at each other all the time. The resort had this janky kayak that Dev, Olivia and I took out in the relatively calm and hopefully sharkless bay. Only two of us could get in it at a time, and we would get the paddling going pretty well, but any slight irregular movement would tip the boat over. It happened again and again. We got to the point where we deliberately tipped it and tumbled into the water because it made us laugh so hard. At times like that, Devlin acted like he was our age, if not younger. Like I said, Olivia and I never had a chance to be alone. Even that evening when we went to the night market in Lamai and tried to be on our own, the parents kept telling us it didn't look like a safe place for us to wander off. I think the people at the resort had told them to watch out for pickpockets. Every time Olivia and I would put a little space between us and the others, one of them would hurry behind us with a comment or a question. "Should we get something to eat?" Or "I saw some souvenirs you might like." So, somewhere, somehow, I made it my goal to kiss Olivia on that last day.

The resort arranged a tour around the island, and, in the first part of the tour, we rattled around in the van on gravel roads until we got to the top of a small mountain. Though the bumpy road was annoying, it had its advantages since Olivia and I shared a seat and kept getting thrown up against each other. I don't mean to be gross, but I got such a boner it was painful. I was thankful she didn't seem to notice. We tumbled out of the van, glad to be back on solid ground. Luckily, I had brought a backpack with water and stuff in it, so I could hold it in front of my crotch without being too obvious.

"Here we are. Buddha's Secret Garden," the guide announced and pointed to a stairway of about a hundred steep steps down the hill. Olivia and I were the first to reach the jungle garden, with weird stone sculptures all around. It was a cool place, which I wanted to appreciate and keep an open mind as my dads had told me to do. But I had one thing in my head: if I wasn't able to share a kiss with Oliva that day, my life would be a total fail.

"Look at these statues, Cole." Every time Olivia said my name, it sent chills through me. Four Thai musicians sat on a large flat rock, two playing traditional stringed instruments, one a flute, and the fourth beating a half circle of drums. The men wore pointed headdresses while nearby a troupe of women dancers positioned at various levels going up the hillside wore the female version of the pointy crown and long silky skirts but were bare-breasted. I stared at the breasts, and even though they were made of stone, it made me wonder what Olivia's breasts looked like. She noticed me staring at the statues and playfully put a hand over my eyes. Maybe she had noticed my erection before. Oh, God.

Another dancer was atop a high stone pedestal above an eagle on a rock with a snake in its mouth. In the background, a chorus of little waterfalls tumbled down the narrow valley, running over figures lying in the middle of the stream.

"What is that supposed to mean?" said Olivia. "Those statues with water flowing over them?"

"I have no idea. It's like they're drowning." I could sympathize. Feeling a little like I was drowning myself.

Steps ran up and down the hills to concrete huts with balconies beside the water, one with a giant stone cobra guarding the entrance. "Let's go up there and look at that snake," I said.

"I'm not terribly fond of snakes."

It obviously wasn't to look at the snake. The little stone house looked like a place we could sneak into and wouldn't be seen by the others.

"It's made of stone," I pointed out somewhat stupidly.

"Yes, but if they use snake imagery, it might mean there

are real snakes about." She was clearly brainy as well as beautiful.

We could hear Dad, a.k.a tour guide, going on as he usually did, gabbing away, and everybody agreeing on what a fantastic place this was.

Our real tour guide had stayed up top, probably not wanting to go up and down all the steps. "Look," said Dad. "It's a village with workers and warriors and royal figures sitting in the middle of all this lush tropical vegetation, palms and bamboo dripping humidity."

"Who created it?" asked Nigel.

"Don't egg him on," I whispered to Olivia, and we giggled.

"This garden was the dream of a durian plantation owner, you know, that fruit of ill repute for its nasty smell but loved by Thais." Dad chuckled. "He started creating his jungle paradise at the age of seventy-seven and continued until he died in his nineties. He brought in sculptors and architects to build it." The excitement in his voice was a little too much.

"Your dad knows quite a lot," said Olivia. Yeah, okay, the place was fly, and I was glad Olivia seemed to enjoy it. But all I could think about was that there had to be some corner where Olivia and I could sneak off to and have our first kiss.

The parents were slowly making their way up and down steps, oohing and awing like they were Alices in Wonderland. Devlin had gone ahead and started jumping from rock to rock, up the sides and back down, back and forth across the stream like a freerunner on a parkour course.

"He's such a show-off," said Olivia. "Let's go up there by the waterfall." Was she thinking the same thing I was thinking?

We climbed up the rocks to a little circular gazebo just above the waterfall, where we could sit on the edge and dangle our feet over the gushing water. Because of the angle the parents couldn't see us, but because of the acoustics, we could hear their conversation perfectly.

"I can't watch him when he does that," said Joanna, referring to Devlin still hopping around.

"I'm more worried about Olivia," said Nigel.

Olivia put her hand over her mouth and giggled. I put a finger to my lips to shush her.

"Colton refuses to talk about it," said Papi. "He acts like nothing is going on."

Joanna laughed. "Devlin didn't have a girlfriend until he was seventeen. He was so involved with sports and school activities."

"He must be popular with the girls," said Dad.

"Terribly," said Nigel. "We asked him if he cared to invite... what's her name, Jo?"

"Zelda."

"Yes, lovely girl. We thought she might want to come with us, but he said no."

"I don't think they're spending as much time together as they were," said Joanna. "Blimey! Look at this place. It's magical."

Olivia took out her phone and earbuds. "Good idea," I said. We plugged in and listened to "Sangria" by Easy Life again, mouthing the words. I held my backpack in my lap, just in case. It felt so great to be sitting close to her and connected by the earphones. When the song ended, I suggested taking a walk and pointed to the woods, the opposite direction from where everybody else was. She nodded and followed me.

We came to a stone bench and sat down. I was sweating like crazy, not hot weather sweat but nervous sweat, the sweat that stinks. Now she'll never want to kiss me. But it was now or never. "Olivia?" She was kicking her feet and staring at the ground. She seemed as anxious as I was.

"Uh-huh."

"Can I...?" Are you supposed to ask? That sounds stupid. I mean British people are so polite.

She reached for my hand. I took that as a go. I leaned in and touched my lips to hers. And then I pulled back a little bit. She touched my cheek, raised her eyes, and smiled. My heart was beating about a hundred miles an hour. "Is that it?" she said.

I shook my head and moved closer. She watched me this time with a sly smile, her lips parted slightly. I smelled her fruity lip gloss. It made me dizzy. "Go on," she said.

A moment later, our mouths were pressed together, and our tongues were cautiously searching. I put my hand on her shoulder and took a clump of her thick hair as if I needed to hold on to something or I would fall off a cliff.

"Olivia!" said Nigel.

We separated quickly, shocked to see Nigel and Papi standing very close by. We had been so into it we hadn't heard their approach.

"Colton, come here!" Papi sounded gruff, but he had this little twinkle in his eyes that he wasn't all that put out.

"Your mum was worried about you," said Nigel, pointing down the path to the lower part of the garden.

Olivia and Nigel walked ahead, and Papi and I followed. He put his hand on the back of my neck, not in a rough way, but showing he was obligated to play the concerned parent role even if he didn't want to. We negotiated the trail and then down over the rocks in silence.

"There they are," said Dad.

Olivia ran over to her mother. "Can't I have any privacy? We weren't doing anything." Joanna looked at Nigel and raised her eyebrows.

Nigel had calmed down from a few minutes before when it looked like he wanted to kill me. "Sweetheart, you can't just pop off like that," said Nigel.

"The guide told us to stay on the path and not wander off," said Papi. "We don't know what's in this area. It could be dangerous."

"Dangerous? Really? I'm not a little kid," I said.

"Don't talk back," said Dad. "Listen to your Papi. From now on, you will always stay where we can see you."

I got that frustrated demon look in my eyes, like I was going to explode. Dad tilted his head and scrunched up his forehead with an eye that said, "You'd better not!"

Devlin stood at the edge of the group but came to the rescue. "Hey, Colton. Come here. I want to show you something."

"Can I?" I said.

"Yes, go," said Dad. "We'll talk about this later. Don't go far. We have to meet the guide back at the van in fifteen minutes."

Joanna grabbed Olivia's hand and suggested they go for a walk to another part of the garden.

As Dev and I walked away, I turned around to see Nigel and my dads huddling like three coaches discussing a game they were losing badly.

Dev put a hand on my shoulder. "Don't worry about it, mate." And then he dropped his hand and narrowed his eyes. "You weren't doing anything..."

"We were just kissing," I said.

"What? You were taking liberties with my little sister. I ought to..."

He looked furious, and I was afraid he might punch me. "I'm sorry. She..."

He raised his hand, and I flinched. Then he clapped it around my shoulders and burst out laughing. "Well done, my man. But nothing beyond kissing, all righty, mate?"

"I promise."

The rest of the tour was awkward. Olivia and I stayed away from each other, only sharing sweet glances and half smiles when no one seemed to be watching. We went to the Wat Plai Laem temple complex on the northern side of the island where there was a huge white statue with lots of arms (I counted eighteen of them) that rose above an island in a lake. On either side were two halls with steep roofs that gave the impression they floated on the water. Dad was happy as always to share his knowledge about the site. "That statue is Guanyin, a bodhisattva believed to be a source of unconditional love and a protector of all beings. The statue should have a thousand arms, but I guess that would be too much for a sculptor." He chuckled. The guide had pretty much given up and become only our driver, letting Dad take over the tour.

"As a protector of all beings, I wonder if she had a hand, or should I say arm, in what was in the news today. Did you see your president was impeached?" said Nigel.

"He won't be removed, though," said Papi. "The senate is too weak-kneed."

"Come on, mates," said Devlin. "No politics today."

I tilted my head and stared at the statue. "Is it a man or a woman?"

"Funny you should ask," said Dad. "Originally in India, Guanyin was portrayed as a man, but later female representations became popular. Many scholars refer to the bodhisattva as androgynous, capable of taking different forms."

"You amaze me," said Devlin. "Your head has the whole encyclopedia crammed inside it."

Dad blushed. "I like to read up on things before I see them."

"What's androgynous?" I asked.

Dad looked at Papi. "Would you like to take this one?"

"Oh, no," said Papi, with a hint of bitterness in his voice. "You're the expert... on everything."

"It means they have both male and female characteristics. Their sex isn't necessarily obvious."

"That's assuming gender is binary," said Devlin. "Many

people now identify as non-binary. Some say there are nine genders."

"I'm not sure I get it," I said.

Nigel patted me on the back. "You and me both."

"Perhaps we should continue this conversation another time," said Joanna.

"Awkward-land! This is where all your research gets us," Papi said to Dad.

Joanna waved at the guide, who stood by the van. "I think it's time for our lunch stop."

Six

It was bad enough that Olivia and I wouldn't see each other for five days, but I started worrying that the parents might cancel our meet up in Chiang Mai like they couldn't trust us not to run off and do a Romeo and Juliet suicide. The night of the tour, my dads sat me down, and I thought, here we go. This had all the makings of bad news, Dad twitching in his seat and Papi sighing.

Dad began. "We understand that you and Olivia like each other and that might lead to certain urges that make you want to take it to the next level. We've talked about sex before, but we need to talk about consent."

Why are you making such a big deal out of this? "We just kissed." I threw my hands up in the air.

"And she was okay with that?" asked Papi.

"Of course."

"We just want to make sure you understand that if you try to kiss or touch a girl and she gives the slightest indication she doesn't want it, you have to stop. Immediately!"

"I know that." Did my own parents think I was some kind of stereotypical Black male predator?

"We hope you do. It's easy to say now, but what about

in a few years when you try alcohol, and we know you will, things could get out of hand, reduced inhibitions, etcetera? No matter what the situation, you have to be absolutely sure there is consent, particularly in your situation."

"What's that supposed to mean?"

"It's because of the image people have of Black men," said Papi in a low, sad voice.

Here it was again. The Black thing. I had this sick, trembly feeling throughout my whole body. I wasn't sure if I wanted to scream or cry. "Is that the image you have of me?"

"God, no," said Dad. "You are a kind, loving, intelligent human being and we trust you. But racism in our society is a sickness that hasn't been cured. I don't want to get all heavy here, but there is a history you need to be aware of."

"Like Josh blaming me for stealing those videos."

"That's different, but, I guess, kind of the same."

I so didn't want to cry, but I could feel the tears welling up. "You're going to cancel our meet up in Chiang Mai, aren't you?" I must have sounded like a five-year-old because I saw sadness in Papi's eyes mimicking mine.

"What? No," said Dad. "We're all looking forward to seeing each other again."

"And her dad?"

"Nigel is a dad who wants to protect his daughter, but he also understands," said Papi with a little chuckle. "He told us a story about Joanna's father slamming the door in his face, saying she couldn't date a white man."

"The other thing is that we are on vacation and you and Olivia live very far away from each other. It's probably not a good idea to get too serious."

"Thanks for reminding me. But you can't just turn your feelings on and off."

Dad and Papi looked at each other as if they didn't have a response for that.

They were particularly nice to me those first five days in Chiang Mai, except they did tease me when I got grumpy about missing Olivia. They didn't get on my case when Olivia and I chatted on WhatsApp constantly while at the same time trying to keep us as busy as possible so my fingers wouldn't fall off from texting so much. They also distracted me by drawing me into researching places where we could spend a day with elephants. We found a good one, but I insisted we wait until the Saxtons could join us.

The day of their arrival finally came, and my dads had torturously decided it would be a good day to visit about five hundred temples. I kept looking at my watch every few minutes, saying, "Isn't it time to go back to the hotel?"

Around five in the afternoon, we entered the hotel lobby, and they were at the counter checking in, surrounded by all their luggage. It wasn't quite the running through fields of sunflowers and falling into each other's arms that I had imagined, but she did separate from her parents, nearly tripping over a small bag, and came over to me, smiling shyly. We hesitated. Then she mouthed, "I fucking hate it when you leave." I had goosebumps up and down my arms about a mile high. We hugged and her hair smelled like a tropical forest. I whispered in her ear, "I missed you."

I looked over her shoulder and saw everyone staring at us. I pulled back and pecked her lightly on the lips.

"Get a room," said Devlin.

"Not funny," growled Nigel. And then we were all hugging and doing continental kisses on each cheek. One big lovefest.

The next day was elephant day. Dad elected to be the one to stay out of the water and film the huge gray wrinkled animals frolicking with nearly naked humans in a shallow pond. The Saxtons, Papi, and I scooped up armfuls of mud and plastered the skin of the elephants lounging in the water. We were introduced to a whole gamut of elephants: old, young, blind, injured from working in the logging industry, and some rescued from the circus. All beautiful. The baby elephants were particularly playful as they bumped against us and sprayed water from their trunks. After all my years of being fascinated with elephants, I was finally able to touch their skin and play with them. And to do it with Olivia nearby filled me with joy.

It was the end of a beautiful day at the sanctuary, the mud bath segment. The guide explained the concept of smearing mud on the elephants to help regulate body temperature and protect their skin against the sun. The young guides also instigated a human mud bath by smearing themselves before playfully doing the same to the tourists. The men had their shirts off and the women wore bathing suits. Olivia had her checkered bikini on, and I wore my favorite board shorts. Devlin became a popular target as it seemed everyone, both male and female, anxiously sought to rub his ripped torso with mud, turning his chocolate skin a baked gray as the muck dried.

After the lecture Papi and Dad had given me about respecting women's bodies, I shyly smeared a little mud on Olivia's arm, but then turned to focus on Papi.

Joanna got out of the water and ran to get her phone. "Augie, you must go in. I'll take over filming now."

Dad took off his shirt and waded into the water. Devlin and I rushed over with fistfuls of sludge. Devlin focused on Dad's chest while I worked on his back. He yelped with the sudden coolness of the mud and water and he seemed particularly delighted in being touched by Devlin. That was weird. Papi stood nearby with his arms akimbo but let out a good-natured laugh. The elephants had been forgotten while the humans were whooping it up.

The guides shouted a command to the animals, getting them to rise out of the water, and the lead guide reminded us we needed to finish rinsing them off with buckets of water.

Life was good. I got to share this mind-blowing experience with Olivia and my dads and Devlin and Joanna, and even Nigel seemed relaxed and not worried I was going to steal his daughter away. At dinner that night, they let Olivia and me sit next to each other, and everyone was nearly giddy with joy as we shared stories from the day. We sat under a canopy of thousands of twinkling lights and hanging ornaments, reminding us Christmas was just a day away. Before the arrival of the Saxtons, we had gone on a one-day excursion to the White Temple in Chiang Rai, a couple of hours away. In the gift shop I had seen a bracelet that I wanted to buy Olivia for Christmas.

Dad looked concerned. "I think it's fine you buy her a Christmas gift, but jewelry is a bit much for a girl you've only known for a few days. Usually, it's something you give a girl once your relationship has progressed." I felt a little anger inside and almost said, "What do you know about buying gifts for girls?" But I realized that was stupid and held my tongue.

Papi agreed with Dad, so, even though I thought the bracelet was perfect for her, I settled on a T-shirt with a sparkly glitter image of Ganesh on the front. I couldn't wait to give it to her, the first gift I had ever bought for a girlfriend, and I paid for it with my savings.

Everyone at the dinner table looked the picture of health, still feeling the effects of the mud bath and elephant experience. Devlin ran his hand up and down his arm. "My skin feels lovely from that mud. Kind of tingly." He looked across the table at Dad and winked. I looked at Papi to see if he noticed.

"You loved to muck around in the mud when you were a child," said Joanna. "Such a dirty little boy." She laughed.

"He's still dirty," said Olivia. "His trainers always stink."

"Rubbish," said Devlin and stuck his tongue out at his sister.

"See what you started, Jo," said Nigel.

"All in good fun," said Joanna. I could see where Olivia got her beauty. But Joanna was so much more than a beautiful woman. She was so warm and often looked at me with this sweet, motherly gaze that tore me up inside. She didn't seem to worry at all that Olivia and I were getting too close. It was a good thing she couldn't see inside my head and the things I wanted to do with her daughter.

In the conversation, Papi not too subtly mentioned he and Dad would be celebrating their anniversary in a couple of days. He tossed a smile in Devlin's direction.

"When did you get married?" asked Joanna.

"That's a complicated question," said Dad. "We tend to celebrate the night we met at a Christmas party seventeen years ago. That's our romantic anniversary because we knew right away it was going to be something. Our actual marriage was so entangled with politics it's hard to pinpoint the date or feel terribly romantic about it. I don't know if it made the news in England in 2004 when Gavin Newsom, then the mayor of San Francisco, ordered the county clerks to start issuing marriage licenses shortly before Valentine's Day, which was a nice touch. We got in line with hundreds of other couples and got our license. Film crews arrived, and we were in a CNN video loop all day. It prompted a ton of phone calls from family and friends, mostly positive. We had a little ceremony in the rotunda of City Hall. A month later, the courts ordered the city to stop issuing of licenses, and our marriage was voided."

"That must have been awful," said Joanna.

"Then in 2008, a couple of years after Colton was born, the Supreme Court of California allowed marriage licenses for same-sex couples. So here we go back to City Hall and get another license, another small ceremony with friends, holding Colton in our arms. That was in May. In November, it was put to a vote by ballot proposition, and the people voted against same-sex marriage. How could anyone look at a picture of our happy little family and not want us to be together?"

"I thought California was one of the most liberal places in the world," said Devlin.

"Coastal California maybe. There are huge sections of Central and Northern California, which are conservative. This time, the marriages weren't annulled, but no new licenses could be issued. We were legally married, but our marriage wasn't recognized in most of the United States. It wasn't until the Supreme Court decision of 2015 that gay marriage was allowed throughout the country."

"What a battle just to marry the person you love!" said Joanna.

"You blokes deserve a night out," said Nigel. "We could take care of Colton for a night. Devlin's got his own room and Colton could bunk with him. That way, you could stay out as late as you like." I was amazed Nigel was suggesting I spend the evening with them, Olivia and me under the same roof.

"That's so kind of you, but really..." said Dad.

"What if I want to go out?" said Devlin.

"Don't be daft, Dev," said Joanna. "They don't want you tagging along. They ought to have a nice romantic evening alone."

Seven

The next morning, Dad, Devlin, and I were the first ones down to breakfast.

"Have you decided where you're going out for your proper romantic evening?" Devlin asked Dad.

"We have a place in mind."

"I wasn't joking about wanting to go out with you gents. Yes, I know you want to have your private dinner and all that, but I could meet you somewhere afterwards for a drink."

"I don't think you'd be interested in where we're going."

"Don't be so sure. What is it? A drag show or something?"

Dad wrinkled his forehead and nodded in my direction as if it was too much for my virgin ears. He got up to refill his plate at the breakfast bar.

Devlin looked at me. "You do know what a drag show is, don't you?"

"Yeah. I think my dads used to do drag for Halloween and stuff."

Dad sat back down. "If you must know, we're going to a place called Ram Bar. They have ladyboy shows. God, that sounds so politically incorrect."

"Cole says you and Ruben used to do drag," said Devlin with a grin.

"Colton! That was way before you were born, and we didn't *do* drag. We dressed up for Halloween."

"It's okay, Dad," I said. "No big deal."

Papi came into the breakfast room, looking like he was still half asleep. Devlin greeted him with a big smile. "Morning, mate, come sit by me." He pulled out the chair next to him, and as he sat down, Devlin put his arm around Papi's shoulders and gave him a morning side hug.

"Augie told me about Ram Bar. Sounds bloody awesome. I know you want to have a proper dinner, but I could meet you there afterwards."

Dad gave Papi an apologetic look. "We don't have to go to the bar. We could make an early night of it."

"Come on, mates. This is your opportunity. Thailand has the best drag shows in the world. I, for one, need a little break from the family." He stood up with his plate. "I'm going to help myself to a bit more of those scrummy eggs."

Dad made a sorry face at Papi. "Are you angry?"

"Do we need a romantic dinner alone? I think it would be more fun to have a dinner celebration with everyone. Then the three of us could go out. What do you think, Cole? Could you manage spending the evening with Olivia?"

"You guys should go." I know Papi's question was sarcastic, but I didn't want to sound too giddy about hanging out with Olivia.

Devlin approached the table step by careful step, putting on a sorry face and pretending to be someone walking into an argument that was his fault.

"Sit down," said Dad, as if he was furious. And then he smiled. "We've got a date."

"Hunky-dory, then?" said Devlin.

Papi gave him a thumbs up. "We're good, mate."

I was a little nervous about spending the evening with Olivia and her parents in their suite, mainly her dad. I felt he was going to have his evil eye on us if Olivia and I even looked at each other. It turned out much better than expected. We played charades, Joanna and I against Olivia and her dad. Nigel was the worst and made us laugh. He couldn't even get the sign for a song right, making it look like he was yawning. After that, we played Uno, where Nigel cleaned our clocks. He was ruthless with the Draw Four cards. We went to bed at one in the morning, Olivia to her parents' room, and I slept in Devlin's room. In the middle of the night, I got up and went to get a glass of water in the little kitchenette off the living room. I sat at the counter and closed my eyes, concentrating on sending a telepathic message to Olivia to come join me. It didn't work, and I went back to bed with the idea it was better to leave well enough alone.

I woke up early and went into the living room. Joanna was making tea in the adjoining kitchen and offered me some. It was a bit awkward at first, but she was nice and acted like she really cared about me. She asked about school and basketball. We didn't talk about Olivia at all. And then she got a little serious.

"Your dad told me you want to meet the woman who gave birth to you."

That was a lot of words to avoid using the word mother. "Yes. I think it would be awesome. She's Black, you know."

"I gathered that," she said with a grin.

"My dads are great, but sometimes I wonder if they really get it."

"You mean what it's like to have dark skin?"

"Yeah. I know it's not easy being gay, but it's different."

"That's true. A gay person isn't necessarily pigeonholed at first sight. They are a minority that can hide, so to speak, not that they ever should. You know I'm a psychologist, right?"

I nodded.

"I imagine you believe your surrogate mom could shed some light on being Black. Help guide you through these difficult teenage years."

"I know my dads don't want her to participate in my life and maybe she doesn't want to, but I just want to talk to her."

"I understand that. And I understand how frustrated teenagers can get with their parents. In the short time I've known your dads, I can say you are one fortunate lad. You are so lucky to have two such loving people in your life."

"I know. I'm not doubting them or disrespecting them in any way. I have lots of friends at school with straight parents, parents who are divorced or mean or majorly messed up in some way. I'm sure I'm way better off with my dads. I just don't have important people of color in my life."

"Well, now you do. Who knows what will happen when we all go back to our normal lives, but I do hope our two families can keep in touch, visit, and grow closer. I would like to help you any way I could."

Wow. Just wow. She would be such a great mom. "Thank you for saying that."

Olivia came in, and though it was fantastic to see her, it ended the conversation with her mom. We sat at the counter and drank tea with lots of milk and sugar in it. We laughed about the game of charades the night before.

"I'm going to go wake up my dads," I said. I was anxious to tell them about my evening with the Saxtons and my conversation with Joanna.

I knocked on the door to our room, but there was no response. I knocked again. After another minute, Dad opened the door. "Hi there, stranger. Did you miss us?"

"Of course I did," I said.

"You did not."

I gave Dad a hug and walked into the room, staring at my empty bed. "Where's Devlin?"

"He's in the bathroom getting dressed."

Dad seemed a little nervous, and though it wasn't unusual for him, I had a feeling of something awkward, maybe having something to do with Devlin being there.

Papi sat on the edge of the big bed with his head in his hands. "Hey, Colie. You're up early."

"What's the matter, Papi?"

"A little headache."

"We played Uno until after midnight," I said. "It was

hella fun."

I guess I was speaking too loudly. "Inside voice," he whispered.

Devlin emerged from the bathroom. "Hey, little bro."

"Hey, Dev."

"See you guys at breakfast. I'm going to take a shower."

Dad made an exaggerated move out of Devlin's path to the door, bumping into a chair and half falling into it. *You guys are acting weird.*

I sat on the bed next to Papi and put my arm around him. "Sorry about your headache."

"Thanks."

"I was just thinking. If Olivia and I got married, Joanna would be like my mom, right?"

"You're fourteen!" said Augie. "Don't be ridiculous."

"Hypothetical, Dad."

"Very hypothetical," said Papi. "Technically, she'd be your mother-in-law."

"And Dev would be like my big brother."

"Uh-huh. Brother-in-law. But you've got a lot of growing up to do before you think about marriage or even dating."

"I know. It's just that Joanna is such a cool lady and Dev is like super cool."

"I thought Olivia was the one you were interested in," Dad teased.

"Duh. She's the most beautiful girl I've ever seen."

Dad sat down next to me. "Do you think she likes you as much as you like her?"

"I don't know. She says she has a boyfriend at home, but it's not serious."

"When we go home, you can keep in touch like on Facebook."

"Facebook? That's for old people. We're on Instagram and WhatsApp. We've already exchanged photos and stuff."

"Well, this old person needs coffee," said Papi. "My head is killing me. Let's go down to breakfast."

While Dad and Papi got ready, I paced the room, opening and closing drawers, fiddling with the remote but not turning on the TV. Sometimes, when I'm nervous or bored, I can't stop myself from fiddling with things. I know it drives my dads crazy, and I was surprised they didn't say anything. Dad seemed preoccupied. He pulled a tank top over his head and stood in front of the mirror, grimacing at his image.

"I talked to Joanna this morning," I said. "Olivia and Nigel were still sleeping."

"What did you talk about?" He removed the tank top and returned to the T-shirt he had started with.

"I told her about wanting to meet my mom. She said she hoped it would happen one day, but I shouldn't worry about it too much."

Dad stopped messing with his shirt and turned to me. "Anything else?"

"She said I was really lucky to have two dads like you guys, and she was sure that when my mom was ready, you would make it happen. Boy, would I love a mom like Joanna."

"We can't choose our parents, but sometimes we get lucky." Dad removed the T-shirt and put the tank top back on.

"I got lucky."

"So did we, buddy," said Papi.

Dad moved close and embraced me. And then he turned up his nose. "Did you take a shower this morning? Brush your teeth?"

I groaned. "Maybe not so lucky."

Dad swatted my butt. "At least brush your teeth."

"Okay, I'll take a shower later out by the pool."

"Just hurry. I need coffee."

I separated from Dad and picked up the remote again. "How come Dev stayed in your room?"

Papi turned his head to look at Dad.

"We got back late," said Dad. "And you were in his bed. At least, that's where I hope you were."

"Aw, Dad. You think Nigel was going to let anything happen?" We all laughed.

Eight

We hurried along Ratchamankha Road with our eyes focused upward where in the distance hundreds of lanterns filled the sky and then drifted off to the east until they became tiny specks of light.

"We're missing it!" I said.

"No," said Papi. "We still have a good hour before midnight. It's only about five minutes away."

We were headed, along with the Saxtons, to the Tha Phae Gate, where the New Year's Eve celebration was scheduled to take place. Our dinner at an Italian Restaurant had taken much longer than expected—a long wait to be seated, and then an hour delay before our pizzas arrived. The creepy Italian owner stalked the restaurant, being mean to the Thai staff, seating and serving his Italian friends before other guests, and, when Dad complained about the long wait, the man answered him rudely. Devlin, who sat next to Augie, said, "Relax, mate. We're on holiday. Have another beer."

"I will, if I can get the waiter's attention."

Joanna turned around, searching for their server. "There's no need for him to be rude. They should have been prepared."

When we eventually got outside, the pizza we had wolfed down sat like a lump in our stomachs as we hurried along the street, now a river of people, foreign and Thai, flowing in the same direction while more partiers poured into the flow from smaller streets and alleys. A street seller had a cart on the corner, loaded down with hundreds of sky lanterns and glow-in-the-dark necklaces we had seen many people wearing. He had a hard time keeping up with all the customers, but Nigel squeezed in and bought a pack of ten lanterns.

He triumphantly returned to the group, holding the bundle of lanterns over his head. "I hope someone has a lighter."

Devlin had moved into his dad's place and negotiated a special price for seven necklaces, each one a different color. "Everybody put on your necklace. Let's line up for a photo."

Olivia and I were frustrated it with the slow adults. "Come on!"

"It'll take a second." Devlin organized us according to the colors of the rainbow and asked a passerby to snap the photo. "We have to share our cell numbers so I can send everyone the photos."

"Great idea!" said Dad.

"You don't have to be so enthusiastic," I heard Papi say in a low voice.

A bunch of fireworks shot up and exploded in the air above us. Olivia grabbed my hand and pulled me toward the explosions. "We're going to miss everything."

"Don't get too far ahead," said Nigel.

The large plaza in front of the Eastern Gate was filled with hundreds of people from all over the world, speaking a variety of languages. I saw women with those scarf things on their heads and long dresses mixed in with European women in halter tops and short shorts.

We weaved through the crowd, and Nigel struggled to keep up with Olivia and me, reminding us he had the lanterns, so we'd better not get lost. On Olivia's right, a bad lantern launch was in progress and Nigel yelled at her to get out of the way. Instead of lifting straight up, the lantern leaned to one side and rose at an angle. I saw what was happening and stepped in front of her to shield her from danger. Ah, yes. Willing to die for my love. The lantern lifted over our heads and went straight toward the trees surrounding the square. A group of young people howled with excitement as the lantern stuck in the branches and burst into flames.

We all turned our heads up, expecting the whole line of trees to catch fire. But, in a short time, the flames died down. "Unbelievable," Dad shouted above all the noise. "I read that the government tried to ban these lantern festivals. Think of the environmental impact and fire danger. I take it they weren't successful. There's no way this would happen in the States, probably not in England, either."

"Oh, Dad," I said. "Can't we just have fun?"

Devlin pinched Dad's elbow. "Yeah, Dad. Don't be a stick in the mud."

Augie glared at him.

We found a space away from the trees and unpacked

the lanterns made of treated paper, a wire frame, with a wax fuel cell on the frame at the open end. Before trying it ourselves, we watched several people light the fuel cell, hold on to the sides of the lantern, one person on each side, until the paper filled with hot air. After a couple of minutes, they let it go. I wasn't the most patient person in the world, so I grabbed the lighter from Devlin's hand and told Olivia to hold on to the other side. The cell didn't light right away, and I burned my hand, dropping the lighter. "Ouch."

"Are you okay, Cole?" said Olivia. "Be careful."

I picked up the lighter and got it lit this time, but we let it go before the lantern filled with air. Instead of going up, it went sideways. The people around us screamed and moved out of the way.

"Colie, we told you to be careful!" yelled Dad.

Of course, Devlin saved the day, chasing it down, pulling it to the ground, and stomping on the fuel cell. He did an exaggerated stomp-dance until the flame went out.

"Kids are so impatient," said Nigel. "All right, Dev, let's show them how it's done." They lit the center, held it until they could feel an upward tug on the frame, and let it go up into the sky. We all clapped.

The pace of rising lanterns increased by the minute, fifty lanterns at a time, and the sky became speckled with hundreds of them. There was little wind, so they didn't drift away rapidly, hanging above us looking like the starry sky that time we went camping with Josh's family in Tahoe. And there was Josh again in my head, who I tried to put out of my mind immediately. I certainly didn't want to think about him when we were having such a stupendous time. Every couple of minutes fireworks shot up and burst in the sky, adding to the festival of lights.

As midnight approached, people held onto their lanterns instead of letting them go. The roar of the crowd grew louder, and a countdown began. Fireworks screamed into the sky, exploding in multiple colors, and then at the stroke of midnight, hundreds of lanterns lifted off at the same time as a cry rose with the lights. My dads let one go, Joanna, Nigel, and Devlin another, and Olivia and I still another. "This is the best night of my life!" I yelled.

"Yes, Colton!" said Joanna. "I have a feeling 2020 is going to be a magnificent year." A firecracker exploded close to her, and she jumped. There was a moment of terror on her face, and then she quickly let out a nervous titter. For the next year, I kept thinking back to her statement that 2020 was going to be a magnificent year. Magnificently sucky!

Dad reached for Papi and they kissed. Nigel and Joanna turned to each other and engaged in a romantic kiss that surprised me, since I hadn't seen them expressing affection before. Olivia and I looked at each other. Well, everyone else was doing it, so we had a kiss that made me feel happy and confident and inspired and hopeful.

"What about me?" asked Devlin.

Dad drew Devlin close and caused a scandal when both he and Papi kissed Devlin passionately on the mouth.

Joanna and Nigel stared at the three men with raised eyebrows. "Hey, mates," said Nigel. "We've got more lanterns to lift off."

It was close to one in the morning when we sent off the last lantern. The crowd had dwindled, and Joanna let out a big yawn. "Had enough, everybody? I know I have."

On the walk back to the hotel, Nigel, Joanna, and Devlin were in front, deep in conversation, Olivia and I held hands in the middle, and my dads brought up the rear. "One more day in Thailand," said Dad as if announcing the end of the world.

I squeezed Olivia's hand, but we didn't say anything.

As we got closer to the hotel, it sounded like Dad and Papi were having a little argument, but I couldn't hear exactly what they were saying.

But I did hear, "The day after tomorrow we'll be on the way home. It will all be a memory."

I wanted to turn around and tell them to shut up. They were bringing me down. Everything had been so perfect.

Dev and his parents stood on the corner, waiting for us. Dev broke away and approached my dads with a big smile. "I just had a chat with Mum and Dad about my taking a little trip before I start my internship at an architectural firm."

"Let me guess," said Papi. "You were thinking about San Francisco."

"I've always wanted to go there. Now I have friends."

Dad had that nervous excitement in his eyes but tried his best to sound nonchalant. "And when were you thinking?"

"The internship starts in April, so perhaps in late February, if we can sort it."

"So next month?" Papi asked.

"Yay," I said. "That's cool." And then I looked at Olivia with a question in my eyes.

"I know that's quite soon, but it's the best opportunity. Unless it's not convenient..."

"Let's discuss it tomorrow on the bike tour," said Dad. "I'm too beat to think about it now."

Olivia let go of my hand and moved closer to her parents. "He's not going without me."

"I was afraid of this," said Nigel. "Olivia, you'll be in school. It's out of the question."

Olivia's shoulders dropped. "Maybe we could all go for summer holidays," she said.

I looked pleadingly at my dads. "Or maybe we could go there, you know, England? That would be cool, right?"

"We'll see." Papi looked over and locked eyes with Joanna. She shrugged, and her eyes seemed to crinkle with doubt.

The next morning at breakfast, everybody tried to act like it wasn't the end of the world, our last full day together. None of us seemed that excited about the bicycle tour, but we had already booked and paid for it.

A van picked us up and drove us to the agency where they fitted us all with bikes and the guide explained we were going to the ruins of an ancient Lanna Kingdom capital, Wiang Kum Kam.

With our guide, we rode along the Mae Ping River on a winding road heavy with traffic in the southern part of

Chiang Mai. Dad kept reminding me not to do some of the little tricks I did at home, like riding hands free. "Drivers here don't respect cyclists in the same way they do at home."

"Yes, Dad." But I still hoped for an opportunity to show Olivia some of my moves.

Dad fell behind the rest of us and missed the signal to turn off the main road onto a smaller one. We waited for him at the turnoff, but he went by us totally in a daze, like he had something on his mind. Papi shouted, and Dad raised his head.

He turned around, caught up to us, and stopped beside where I straddled my bike with my arms crossed. "And you're always getting on my case for not paying atten-tion," I said with a big grin.

Dad apologized to the group.

"No problem," said Jen, the chunky male guide with calves the size of tree trunks from leading so many bike tours. "Maybe you need drink more water. We stop soon." It was hella hot like it had been everywhere in Thailand, but I had a feeling that wasn't Dad's problem.

From the smaller road, we turned onto a gravel lane lined with bamboo. The tall stalks leaned toward the middle of the way, forming a canopy that turned the light into a cool pale green, giving us a break from the heat. We stopped for water and a snack, but Devlin and I had other ideas. We raced to the end of the alley, squeezed the brakes, causing the wheels to spin out, and then raced back to where Olivia stood, clapping.

Jen smiled. "These brothers have fun together. Must

love too much."

"They're not brothers," said Joanna. She pointed at me. "He's Augie and Ruben's son. They're American and we're British."

"Oh, I see," said Jen, though his blank stare made us wonder if he did.

I took off again and threw my hands in the air to ride hands free. In the next second, I had toppled over onto the ground. Dad and Papi hurried over to me.

"Are you okay?" said Papi.

I examined my skinned knee. "I'll survive. It was pretty cool though, right? I would have been fine if the tire hadn't gotten stuck in a rut."

As soon as Dad realized my injuries were minor, he had to get all serious. "That's what you get, trying to impress, but now you look ridiculous. These aren't our bikes, you know. If they're damaged, we have to pay for them."

I looked behind them and smiled. Olivia was on her way over. "Are you all right, Cole?"

"I need you to help me up since all my dads want to do is give me a hard time."

She leaned over and inspected the knee, wincing as if she felt my pain, and then delicately brushed the dirt from it. She took her water bottle from her belt loop and poured some over my wound. I was in heaven.

We got back on a busy road that crossed over the river but soon turned again onto a smaller road that weaved through a quiet suburban area where people went about their normal lives of tending small gardens, going shopping at the local markets, and sweeping the patios of their houses. A few dogs got up and ran out to the road to bark at us, and we raised our legs like they were going to bite them off. But most of the dogs barely raised their heads to note our passing. Everything was all normal country living with neighborhoods of small simple houses, and then, suddenly, we saw a tall white monument rising up much higher than any of the other buildings like something you might see in a futuristic movie. "Wat Chedi Liam," Jen shouted.

It was shaped like a pyramid with five tiers of dozens of arched niches holding Buddha statues. There was a single golden spire on top and one at the corner of each level. On every corner of the base was a stone lion.

We pulled over at the foot of the structure and got off our bikes. While everyone else stared up in bewilderment, looking like typical tourists, I discovered a row of hanging bells of different sizes and shapes and proceeded to ring each one several times, going up and down the row. I mean, they had little wooden sticks on string next to each one, so I assumed they were supposed to be rung. Dad looked at me with disapproval. "What?" I said.

"No, it's okay," said Jen. He talked about the good luck from ringing the bells, but promptly added if you rang them too much it might bring bad luck. Oops. During the rest of the tour, the guide constantly returned to the theme of good and bad luck. A little later, we stopped at a huge banyan tree with branches fanning out in all directions. Propped against the tree were hundreds of forked poles, fashioned from branches to look like large crutches. Some of them appeared to support outlying branches, but most of them only leaned against the trunk. Medallions of flat gold-colored metal in the shape of leaves had been tied to the poles with colorful ribbons, and on the medallions, messages were written with a marker. Dad spotted one in English that read, "Protect my son from the evil ways." He showed it to me.

"Did you write that one, Dad?" We laughed and showed Papi.

"People who bring these poles will have big good luck," Jen explained. "Because they support the tree. But also you can have luck if you make a donation over there and write a message on the leaves."

When no one made a move to purchase a metal leaf, he laughed. "Don't worry. I have other way you can get good luck today."

Jen led us to a part of the complex with a smaller chedi topped with a golden dome and spire. With a big smile he said, "This very good luck. You must follow steps correctly or bad luck. First, most important, you make do-nation to temple." He indicated the offering box, and then demonstrated how you ladled water into a silver bowl suspended from a cable. Attached to the cable above the bowl was an ornately worked golden rooster. "Now you make a wish. The wish goes into the water. Then you pull cable to send water to top of chedi. Inside is some relic of Buddha." Jen demonstrated the process, and the bowl rose with the rooster bouncing on the cable while Thai music played in the background through the temple complex speakers. When the bowl was almost to the top, it tipped, sending the water spilling over the façade. "Beautiful, right?" said Jen. He nodded to Olivia. "Young lady go first. Daddy make the offering."

Nigel reluctantly stuffed some bills into the box.

"I know what I'm wishing for." She smiled at me.

Jen held up his hand. "Don't say. You have bad luck and don't get wish."

Each of us had a turn at the water spilling operation with no one declining for fear we would have bad luck.

With our good fortunes assured at least for the next month, we left our bikes in a parking area and walked through the archeological zones where the red brick foundations of numerous temple buildings and chedis were visible. A bit of imagination allowed us to envision the former city.

"This used to be the capital of the Lanna Kingdom, right?" said Dad, never missing an opportunity to show what he knew. "Then they moved it to Chiang Mai."

"That is correct," said Jen. "I just going to say that."

Devlin put a hand on Jen's shoulder. "Don't worry. He's like an encyclopedia."

Papi let out a harrumph.

Jen announced it was time for lunch and led us to a rustic open-air restaurant with rough wooden tables and stools. "Everybody can eat the pork meat?" When we all nodded, he went to consult with the cook.

We sat down at a large table and watched Jen talking to the cook in her basic and possibly unsanitary open kitchen. She swatted away flies while she stirred a large pot, and scraps of food dotted the ground around it.

"I hope this isn't our last meal together," said Joanna. "I

would like something a little more celebratory."

Dad laughed. "I hope this isn't our last meal, period."

"I think we should be okay if we stick to cooked food. No salad," said Nigel.

Devlin shook his head. "You all worry too much. I've eaten lots of street food here in Thailand and I've never gotten sick."

A few minutes later, a young woman came to our table with bowls of steaming soup. It was a grayish broth with vegetables and a few chunks of pork. Devlin was the first to dive in. "It's quite tasty."

Olivia turned up her nose. "I'm not hungry. It looks awful."

"At least try it, Livie. You'll need your strength for the ride back."

"I would love an order of fish and chips right now," said Olivia.

"Me too. I love fish and chips," I said.

Olivia's mood had changed in a second. "I doubt you've ever had a proper fish and chips." She spoke with a bite in her voice, making it sound like a putdown. I felt the sting, and it made me feel all squiggly inside.

"I'll take a good burger and fries any day," said Devlin. "I don't know why you call them French fries, though."

"Why can't you call them chips like we do?" said Olivia. "Americans always have to do things their own way."

"Livie!" said Joanna. "What's got into you?"

Olivia got up from the table. "You're all unbearable." Even me? She walked out of the restaurant toward where we had parked the bikes. Joanna stood up and followed her.

Devlin looked at me. "Don't worry, mate. It's not you. She gets like that sometimes." I tried to act like it didn't bother me despite the fact that a short time before she had been my Florence Nightingale (we learned about her in history class), attending to my knee and sharing the pain I felt and now was treating me like an American troglodyte. That's my new favorite word. Once Nana, Dad's mom, got so frustrated with her son-in-law, Bart, she called him a troglodyte, which sounded funny, especially when Dad explained what it was.

Papi cleared his throat and announced to the table. "I made a reservation at Dash, a highly recommended restaurant, for tonight. I forgot to tell you."

"For all of us?" said Devlin.

Papi thought for a minute and then got a sly grin on his face. "Uh... the maximum table size is six. You wouldn't mind eating on your own, would you?"

"Wicked! I'm cut to the quick," said Devlin.

"Papi? What?" I said. I was already upset about Olivia, and now this. "If Dev's not going, I'm not either."

"He's kidding, Colie," said Dad.

Devlin put his arm around me. "Thanks, my brother."

The attention turned to Nigel when he made a loud slurping noise with his soup. He put down his spoon, grabbed a paper napkin, and wiped his mouth. His face turned red. "I've never enjoyed eating soup in public. How does one do it without causing a racket?"

Nine

It was still dark when we rolled our bags into the hall-way of the hotel and closed the door on our Thai holiday. I was groggy from having to get up so early and in general feeling pretty awful. Olivia had been acting strange the day before. Throughout the rest of the bike tour and at the final dinner at Dash, we barely spoke. In the evening, our two families had said goodbye in the hotel lobby, everybody hugging and promising to stay in touch. Olivia and I hugged, but no kiss. I had no idea what was going on. When my dads and I had gotten on the elevator and the door began to close, I mouthed the words of our song to her, but she looked away. I didn't know if we would ever see each other again. If that wasn't bad enough, in a couple of days, I would be going back to school and the uncertainty of what would happen with my former two best friends. And though I had been distracted from my quest of meeting my mother, I had been thinking about it more after my talk with Joanna. Maybe Joy would be as cool and wonderful as Olivia's mom, in which case I definitely wanted to meet her.

I yawned loudly and glanced down the hall. Olivia was sitting on the floor, gripping her knees with her head bowed. My heart about jumped out of my chest. When the door closed, she jumped up. I dropped my bag and ran to her. We fell into each other's arms and she whispered, "I'm sorry," in my ear, which made me shiver all over.

"Me too," I said.

"You have nothing to be sorry for. It was me."

She had tears running down her cheeks and she had morning breath, but I didn't care. I kissed her and hugged her tight.

"Colton, we have to go," said Dad.

"Text me when you get to Hong Kong," she said. We had a twenty-four-hour layover in Hong Kong before flying home.

"You won't forget me?" I said, sounding a little desperate.

"No way."

"I gotta go." We kissed again.

"Colie, come on," said Papi in a loud whisper.

I rejoined my parents but looked back at her several times and waved as we waited for the elevator.

Papi put his arm around my shoulders. "Are you okay?"

"Yeah."

The elevator dinged, and the door slid open. I shouted, "I fucking hate it when you leave."

"Yes!" she yelled back.

"Colton!" said Dad. "What the hell was that?"

"Sorry. It's a line from our song."

We got on the elevator and I almost got my head crushed as I leaned out to wave to her one more time.

"That's your song?" said Dad. "With that kind of language."

But when he saw how bad I felt and the tears in my eyes, he let it go. Both my dads moved close and put their arms around me. I felt better knowing how much they loved me and that maybe Olivia did, too. Maybe a little bit?

The flight to Hong Kong and the twenty-four hours we were there was a big blur. I had so much on my mind. My dads' answer to that was to cram in as many of the tourist sites as we could—the Star Ferry from Kowloon where the hotel was to Hong Kong Island, the Tram ride to Victoria Peak, the Ten Thousand Buddhas Monastery with its four hundred steps lined with golden statues, and dinner in the Lan Kwai Fong district. Because of violent protests over the past year, there were few tourists and no lines at the places of interest. We commented on the fact that so many Hong Kong residents wore masks in the streets. When we got back to the hotel, Dad asked the hotel desk clerk why.

"People wear mask in winter when there is the flu and bad air in the city."

"So, it has nothing to do with the reports of an outbreak of pneumonia cases in Wuhan?" Dad asked. We had watched BBC news in the hotel and heard a brief report about it.

The clerk looked confused and stared at the computer screen in front of him. "No. People always wear the mask here. It is good hygiene."

Despite the assurance from the clerk, we were happy

to land in San Francisco and be far away from China.

At dinner on Sunday night after arriving home in the afternoon, Dad made an announcement after doing some research on the Internet. "They're calling this thing corona virus, and the first case outside of China has just been reported in, wait for it, Thailand!"

"No way!" said Papi.

I jumped up. "I'd better go call Olivia to make sure she's okay."

"After dinner, Cole," said Dad. "Are they back home now?"

"They got back last night."

"I'm glad we're home," said Papi. "It feels like we've dodged a bullet."

"I haven't forgotten your promise about going to LA," I said. "So I can meet my mom."

Dad sighed. "I imagine Papi has used all his vacation time, and you missed several days of school already this year."

"What about President's Day week?"

"That might work," said Papi.

I could tell from his expression Dad felt pressured again, and he wasn't going to get out of it. He agreed that we would go to Los Angeles and the rest would be up to Joy. Papi said he would contact her and let her know. I had one little victory, but another challenge awaited me when I went back to school the following day.

I didn't see Josh or Fer during the day, but when I got to the locker room for practice, everyone was talking about Josh. His father had pulled him out of Mission, and he was enrolled in a private school, Cathedral Prep. I was still pissed at him, but I also felt a tiny bit sorry for him, having to leave school in the middle of the year. At least I didn't have to worry about any awkward meetings in the halls. While all the guys were expressing their surprise and giving their opinions, Fer remained silent and was the first one out on the court.

We went through our usual drills, and Coach kept yelling at us for how out of practice we were. At the end we had a little scrimmage, and I was guarding Fer. He knocked into me hard, and I landed on the floor. I thought he had done it on purpose, and I wanted to get up and punch him in the face, even though it might have gotten me suspended from the team. But then he reached out his hand and helped me up. "Sorry, man." He pulled me up with such force our chests bumped, and for a split second, we were eye to eye. He whispered, "I screwed up. See you after."

"Everything okay over there?" said Coach.

"Yeah, we're good," I said.

Fer and I met on 18Th Street and started walking home without saying a word. I could tell he was struggling with what to say.

"Look, what I said that day was messed up," he began. "I didn't mean any disrespect to you or your dads."

"My dads?"

"Well, I mean, it was like I was saying you were gay. Seriously, I could care less if you were. I talked to Blanca about it." Blanca was his girlfriend. "She said I was a jerk."

"Does she think I'm gay?"

"No. But she wouldn't care either. I just want us to be friends again."

"I'm not... gay. I met this girl in Thailand."

He smiled and punched me on my arm. "You like Asian girls?"

I laughed. "No, dude. She's British. She was on vacation, too, with her family. She's Black, well, mixed like me."

"So, do Black people there talk all British and shit?"

"Pretty much. Let me show you a picture." I pulled out my phone and showed him a pic of Olivia in her red checkered bikini.

"Seriously, dude. You got that pic of some model off the Internet and are trying to pretend she's your girlfriend."

"Nope. I would show you our steamy texts, but I wouldn't want to corrupt your virgin eyes."

"Come on. Give it to me straight. That awesome chick is your girlfriend?"

"We kissed and everything. I think we're going to London in the summer. Our two families hung out together."

He was genuinely so happy for me he stopped and pulled me into a hug. "Hey," I said, "so you're not breaking up with me?"

"Now you're the jerk." We were getting close to Mission Street. "You wanna stop for some tacos?"

"I could eat about ten of those."

"I'm a bit low on the moolah."

"Don't worry. I gotcha."

I felt this huge weight off my shoulders. We didn't even mention Josh the rest of the time we spent together. I left him at his house and felt so good I started to skip down the street to mine but caught myself after a couple of seconds. I had just claimed I wasn't gay, so I'd better not give anybody the wrong idea.

Ten

The Airbnb we rented was a cottage behind a large Spanish-style house in West Hollywood, a couple of blocks from Santa Monica Boulevard. Papi was excited to be in Southern California where he grew up, staying a short distance from the clubs where he had been for a few years a party boy. "Before I met Augie," he assured me.

"I bet you were really popular," I said. "Did you have lots of boyfriends?"

"All right," said Dad. "Enough of that."

I was a bundle of nervous energy at the prospect of meeting my mother. On the night before we left, I talked to Olivia about it on a WhatsApp call. I told her how Joy was a singer, and she was working on an album, though, okay, I made the last part up.

Joy suggested lunch at this Mexican place on Santa Monica, which she described as a quirky taqueria and agua fresca bar. We arrived first, and my dads ordered margaritas, and an horchata for me. A half-hour late, Joy made an entrance as if she was walking on stage to hella applause. My eyes about popped out of my head at how beautiful she was. Her head was wrapped in a red turban to match the red in the knee-length dashiki she wore over a pair of tight jeans. Dangling earrings caught the light while her wrists were heavy with metal and beaded bracelets. She was like an African queen, and I felt so proud.

Her entrance was so striking we almost didn't notice a shorter, brown-skinned woman who looked to be about ten years younger follow her into the restaurant. She had short-cropped hair and multiple ear piercings. We stood up from the table and Joy introduced her friend as Simone. Simone's eyes darted around like she wasn't too pleased at the awkward gathering. Dad was immediately tense. I could feel my initial excitement fading away. Please, Dad, don't ruin this for me.

Dad and Papi had told me they hadn't seen Joy since the day I was born, though Papi had talked to her several times over the years. They had all agreed it would be best not to have contact, but Papi didn't like the idea of not being in touch with his old friend and biological mother of his child. Every few years he would track her down, and they would talk. In the time after my birth, she lived in Los Angeles, followed by several years in New York, and then there was a period of time they had no idea where she was. A few years ago, Papi had learned she was back in Los Angeles. I know the music industry is tough, and she was probably working really hard to make it.

Joy turned to me and shook my hand. "My, what a handsome young man you are! How old are you now?" That really threw me. I think you were there when I was born.

But I forced myself to smile. "Uh... fourteen."

I hoped she wouldn't ask when my birthday was because Dad looked like he was ready to have a fit.

"What? You two never met?" said Simone. Her eyes twinkled.

Papi let out an uneasy chuckle. "They met on the day of his birth."

Dad waved his hand toward the table. "Let's all sit down. I guess we'll need another chair. We didn't know you were bringing someone extra." His voice had a bite to it. Come on, Dad, be nice.

"She's not extra. She's my partner."

"It would have been nice to know."

Joy ignored the comment and grabbed the two nearest chairs on one side of the table for her and Simone. Papi asked the people at the next table if he could take a chair while I stood dumbfounded, not knowing where to sit.

"Why don't you sit here, Colie?" Dad indicated the chair at the end of the table.

I groaned. "I wish you'd stop calling me that." Now that I had a girlfriend and was meeting my mother, I had asked my parents not to call me Colie anymore.

Joy rose up in an exaggerated stiff-backed posture. "Colie does sound a little childish for a young man like you."

"My girlfriend calls me Cole. I like that," I said.

"Oh, you have a girlfriend."

"Yeah, I met her in Thailand."

Simone let out a disapproving "Hah."

"A girlfriend in Thailand? So far away," said Joy.

"Noooo. She's British. She lives in London. I mean, that's far away, too, but we talk every day."

Simone put her hand over her face to stifle a giggle. We were definitely not off to a good start.

The server came and took our orders.

"Joy, do plan to stay in Los Angeles?" asked Dad.

She looked at Dad suspiciously, as if she wanted to ask him what business it was of his. But she steadied herself and took a breath. "We're not sure." She looked at Simone and smiled. "We might move to Miami. Simone has some connections in the music industry. Her family knows Gloria Estefan's family."

"Florida? Really?" said Dad. He continued in his unfriendly tone.

"What's wrong with Florida?" said Joy.

"Too many Republicans. Too many people who will vote for Trump." Here we go.

Joy flashed Simone a warning look, as if hoping she would keep quiet.

Simone leaned forward with a big smile. "I kind of like the guy. At least he won't let the socialist Democrats take control. My parents risked their lives, gave up everything to come to this country and leave the socialismo o muerte bull of Castro behind."

Dad nodded his head. "You're Cuban. Now it makes sense. You're the people who would trade one dictator for another."

"You know nothing of the terrible suffering in Cuba."

"Do you? Have you been there? You were born here, right?"

"Yes, I was born in this country, land of freedom thanks to people like Donald Trump."

"Don't make me laugh. He believes in freedom for people like him, and, sister, believe me, you're not in his group." Please, Dad. Let it go.

"Everybody chill out," said Papi. "We're not here to discuss politics. This lunch is about Colton meeting his... uh... Joy."

The food arrived, and they ordered more margaritas. A Mariachi band entered the restaurant and started with a yip, yip, yip, and blaring horns. They played one song next to a center table and then headed directly to ours, almost as if the band had detected some bad mojo at our table and planned to drown it out.

When they moved on, everyone let out a sigh of relief. The music was extremely loud.

"FYI," said Joy. "Simone and I don't always share the same political opinions. We agree to disagree."

"Sometimes we just plain disagree," said Simone.

"Ruben and I agree to disagree on the best pizza toppings or even where Colton should go to school. But we're in absolute agreement we don't want four more years of this madman in office. It's not about politics. It's about decency."

"Augie, please," said Papi.

Dad stood up abruptly. "Excuse me." He scanned the room until he saw the sign for the restrooms. He grunted and pointed in that direction. We all let out a sigh of relief.

Joy turned to me. "Cole, honey, how's everything in school?"

"All right, I guess. Are you really thinking of moving to Miami?"

"Too soon to say. I sent a demo tape to Estefan Enterprises. That's Gloria Estefan's company. Do you know who she is?"

"I don't think so. Maybe I've heard of her."

"She's a big deal."

"That's so cool. I wish I could hear you sing."

"Oh, you will."

While Dad was in the bathroom, Simone said she had to leave. When he came back and saw her empty seat, he made a questioning sign to Papi.

"She left," Papi said, with a little anger in his voice.

"It's my fault?"

"It wasn't the time or place."

"Do you have a picture of your girlfriend?" Joy asked me.

I pulled up a photo on my phone, the same one I had shown Fer. "This one is by the pool at the resort where we met."

"Oh, my goodness. She's like us. When you said British, I thought..."

"Her mom is Black, and her father is white. The guy in the background is her brother. He's super cool."

She was beaming and glanced at Dad with a strange look. "Sounds like you had a wonderful time. I've never even been out of the country. I'm glad you have advantages I never had." She picked up her phone to look at the time. "I have to leave soon. What are you doing tomorrow?"

"I think we're going to Universal Studios," I said. "Maybe you can come with us."

"That sounds like fun, but I have some studio time booked. A different kind of studio," she said with a laugh.

"What about the following day?"

"I have to work."

"I thought it was a holiday."

"Not in the restaurant where I work."

You knew I was coming, and you couldn't have saved a little time for me? "Well, it was nice to meet you."

"I'm thrilled to meet you. Next time you all come down, I'll make sure I have more time." She didn't sound terribly convincing.

"I hope I didn't upset Simone," said Dad, almost sounding sincere.

"Heavens, no. She's tough. She gets into it with a lot of my friends."

"Can I call you sometime?" I said.

Joy hesitated a couple of seconds too long. "Oh, sure. Why not? Ruben has my number. Here, let me give you a hug."

She held me close for a long embrace. I took in her perfume and the warmth of her body, the body I was inside for nine months. It was the strangest feeling. I kind of felt like crying, but I was also a little angry with her.

I think Papi understood how uncomfortable I was and stepped close. "Joy, can we give you a ride somewhere?"

"No, thanks. I'm walking over to the Beverly Center. I'm meeting Simone over there, and we're going shopping." She gave Papi a hug. "You've raised a fine young man. I knew you would."

Dad stood at a distance, probably wondering if she was going to hug him too. She turned to him. "I haven't forgotten you." Their embrace left a lot of air between them. And then she was gone.

As we walked to the car, I said, "That was weird."

"What do you mean?" said Papi.

"Everything. And you didn't help, Dad."

"I'm sorry. I should have kept my mouth shut."

"Simone wasn't very nice," I said. "And how could she like Trump?"

"Don't worry about it. You got to meet Joy," said Papi. "That's what you wanted." Leave it to Papi to try and put a positive spin on it.

"She hugged me, at least."

"Of course she did," said Dad. "I'm sure she's thought a lot about you since the day you were born. She must be proud of the person she helped create."

"She could have sent a birthday card or something."

Dad put his arm around me. "How about a drive to the ocean? We can go out on the Santa Monica Pier."

Eleven

The day after the lunch with Joy, we went to Universal Studios and then in the afternoon went to visit Papi's brother in East LA, the only one of his four siblings who still lived in the Los Angeles area. His parents had recently moved back to Leon, Mexico. They had worked extremely hard over the years and, little by little, built a house in the countryside outside Leon for their retirement. Papi's littlest sister has Down Syndrome, so she went with the parents. The other two sisters married and moved away, one to Seattle and the other to Atlanta. From time to time, we used to get together with the whole family in the house where his brother now lived.

From bits of conversation over the years, I had the impression Papi's parents weren't thrilled to have a gay son with a Jewish husband, and then a Black grandchild. When I asked about it, my dads were mostly truthful, but I could tell it was a topic Papi preferred to stay away from. He assured me they got over their prejudices and made Dad and me welcome. And I remember mostly happy times with his family. We would eat a lot of wonderful Mexican food made by his mom, listen to ranchero music, and dance. Sometimes it seemed like the whole block was one big party and neighbors would wander in and out. One time, when I was about six, I wandered off or went with one of my cousins to a house down the block. I don't remember how I got there, but suddenly I was aware I was in a strange house and didn't recognize anybody around me. People were looking at me funny. Of course they were. About 99.9% of the people for blocks around were Latino. All the restaurants were Mexican or Salvadorean. All the markets and stores had Spanish names. Everyone spoke Spanish. I was a little Black boy that fallen out of the sky. The music was loud, and I began to cry.

Dad and Papi had panicked and run all over the neighborhood, sure I had been kidnapped. And then, after what seemed like a really long time, I looked up and saw Dad standing in the doorway of the house and everybody nearby pointing at me. I ran to him and buried my face in his stomach.

I never got to know my cousins that well, but they were cool except for the mildly racist things they used to say to me: Can I touch your hair? Why are the palms of your hands so white? Let's dance. I'm sure you're a good dancer. Are you going to be the next LeBron?

One of the reasons Papi's parents returned to Mexico was that they weren't happy with the direction the neighborhood was going. Each time we went to visit, we noticed more houses with security doors and bars on the windows. It seemed like there were fewer parties and neighbors didn't wander from house to house anymore. Papi's brother told us East LA was one of the few areas of Los Angeles actually losing population. The gangs had ruined things.

On this trip to Los Angeles, Dad didn't particularly want to visit Uncle Alfonso, but Papi said he couldn't go to LA and not visit his brother. "Okay," said Dad, "as long as we leave before dark."

We had a barbecue in the backyard. The two younger kids, much younger than me, were there, but the two teenage kids had other things to do. It was a little annoying they chose to ghost their cool Black cousin from San Francisco, but the teenage years are weird. Believe me, I know. It wasn't like the parties of the old times. I was bored and kept checking my phone so often for messages from Olivia that my dads threatened to take it away again. We got out of there before dark, but just barely, because to leave a Latino gathering it's usually at least a half hour from the time you first say you're going to leave to actually getting out the door.

To be honest, I wasn't terribly sad to be leaving Los Angeles and going home. I still had a strange feeling in the pit of my stomach about the meeting with Joy, and the visit to Papi's family wasn't much fun. We landed at SFO, and a funny thing happened when we were waiting for the BART train. I looked down the platform and saw a woman that looked like Aunt AJ. Since Aunt AJ was a mouthful, she was perfectly cool with me calling her AJ. She was the youngest of Dad's three siblings.

"Is that AJ?" I asked.

Dad looked in the direction I was pointing. "You're right." We walked toward her.

When we got close, I called out her name. She looked at first shocked and then embarrassed.

"What are you doing here?" said Dad.

"Coming back from a little trip. And you?"

"We were in Los Angeles," I said. "I met my mom." I tried to show enthusiasm, but I guess my smile looked forced.

She raised her eyebrows at Dad, and said, "Oh."

"We had lunch with her," said Papi, all cheery, putting on the spin. "It was casual, you know, a preliminary meeting. She looked great."

"She said she'd have more time to spend with us next time," I said.

AJ wrinkled her brow, searching for another subject. "I hear you have a girlfriend."

"Yeah," I said. I had no problem being enthusiastic about that. "We're going to England in the summer to see her."

"Oh, really?" said AJ.

"We'll see," said Dad. He touched AJ's arm. "Wait a minute. A little trip where?"

A man walked by wearing a mask like we had seen a lot of people doing in Hong Kong. "Augie, look at that guy over there in the mask," said AJ. "He sat right in front of me on the plane and wiped down the area of his seat with sanitary wipes. He wore a mask the whole way. I don't know if he's a germaphobe or knows something."

"What? Are you coming back from Wuhan, China?"

"Very funny. But his behavior must have something to do with the virus everybody's talking about."

"AJ! Where were you?"

She twisted her mouth like she could either lie or tell the truth but knew Dad wouldn't believe a lie. "Uh... Mexico City."

"You didn't."

"I did."

"You in danger, girl," said Dad.

"Why is she in danger?" I asked.

"I was kidding."

"Maybe not," mumbled AJ.

Whenever the topic of AJ and Mexico came up, everybody acted like there was a mystery they couldn't talk about in front of me. Every time I asked about it, they were evasive. After Nana died, Dad and his three siblings went to Puerto Vallarta without their spouses and kids, something about being together and celebrating Nana's life without distractions. The second time Dad called from Mexico, Papi's face went from smiling to unsmiling in about a second, and he said he couldn't talk because I was sitting right next to him. There were several calls with his mamá, and then a conversation in Spanish with an uncle in Mexico. I was dying to know what was going on, but all Papi would say was that Dad was fine and would be home in a few days. When we went to the airport to pick up Dad, M and Lio, AJ wasn't with them. The only thing I could get out of my dads was that AJ needed more time away because she and her husband, Bart, were having problems. Now she was coming back from another trip to Mexico that nobody seemed to know about.

It was the hour when a large number of flights arrived around the same time, making the crowd waiting for

BART several people deep along the platform. When the train arrived, everybody pushed ahead of us, and we were left without seats. Papi and I got separated from Dad and AJ. It looked like Dad and AJ were sharing secret information, smiling and laughing. "What's going on, Papi?"

"I don't have a clue," he said.

"But there's something about AJ and Mexico that no one will tell me."

"We'll tell you someday."

Suddenly, Dad gave AJ a big hug, and they both jiggled with laughter.

"Let's move closer," I said to Papi. "I think we're missing out."

"Curiosity killed the cat," said Papi.

"But the cat..."

"I know... had nine lives."

AJ raised her eyebrows as we move closer to them. "To be continued," she said.

Dad looked at his watch. "Don't you have the boys this weekend?"

AJ and Bart were now divorced. She had two sons, Jason and Elijah. Jason was a year older than me and Elijah a year younger.

"Bart's dropping them off. Lio's at my house in case I don't get back before they arrive." Lio was another of Dad's siblings, a couple of years older than AJ. His full name was Julio because, you know, it's such a common Jewish name. Really, Dad's family was the least Jewish of any Jews I had met, not that I knew much about it. Even

Nana and Pops, who had both passed, didn't celebrate Jewish holidays or go to temple. Dad's family name, Burd, which most people misspelled like Bird or Byrd, hardly sounded Jewish.

Papi's last name was Paniagua. I had a hyphenated last name. Colton Burd-Paniagua. A mouthful, I know, but it has a nice ring to it. Every time I started a new school year or had a substitute teacher, they would get through the first two parts just fine, but they would stare in horror at the third. It would usually come out something like Panny-a-goo-ah. But once you got it, it rolled off your tongue. Pah-ni-ah-gwah. Sometimes when Dad introduced his husband or me to a stranger and the stranger would make a comment like, "That's an interesting name," Dad would go off on his spiel (I learned that and a bunch of other cool Jewish words from Nana). He would explain that it meant bread and water in Spanish. And then he would talk about how bread and water was traditionally used in prisons and on navy ships as a form of punishment because it was enough to keep someone alive, but after a while, the prisoner would start suffering from nutritional deficiencies like Vitamin A. It wasn't until 2019 that the U.S. Navy officially banned the practice of using bread and water rations as a form of punishment. At that point, the listener's eyes would start glazing over and Papi would clear his throat. Dad could have gone on about how in Spanish they put an 'i' instead of a y in front of a vowel, so Paniagua was spelled with an 'i'.

One time, Papi had had enough and said, "Augie, do you feel like a prisoner living with Paniagua?"

Dad was momentarily stunned but recovered quickly and laughed. "Good one. Was I going off?"

"Yes," Papi and I said at the same time.

Someone getting off the BART train bumped into me, pushing me closer to AJ. She smiled and put a hand on my shoulder to steady herself. "Colie, tell me about your girlfriend."

"He prefers Cole now," said Dad.

"Oh, okay. Now that you're all grown up." She gave me a squeeze on the shoulder and then pulled me into a hug. "You are taller and more handsome every time I see you. You're going to have lots of girlfriends. What's her name?"

"Olivia. She's so pretty and has the coolest accent. We like the same music."

We told her all about the trip to Thailand because we hadn't had a chance to get together since we had gotten back. She had been going through a hard time with the divorce. She and Bart used to live in Modesto, but she moved back to Oakland, where Dad and his siblings had grown up. Since she and Bart shared custody, she was constantly driving back and forth to pick up or deliver the boys.

We got off at the 24th Street Mission station with promises to get together soon while AJ stayed on the train to go across the bay to Oakland.

There had been a time when Dad's relationship with AJ had been strained mainly because of Bart and an incident that had happened with me and my cousins. It was about four years ago when Nana and Pops were alive. Dad's siblings and spouses and kids used to get together on Sundays at the big fancy family home in the Rockridge area of Oakland. They had a huge backyard with lawn furniture, a large table under an umbrella, and a grassy area where we played games like croquet and horseshoes. The difference between those gatherings and the ones in East LA were was like night and day. Another big difference was that Nana and Pops didn't need a probationary period before they accepted me. Dad said they loved me from the first moment they saw me. Considering how ugly I looked in those first pictures, they were truly warm-hearted and accepting people.

Pops loved horseshoes, and, as a matter of fact, had a heart attack while playing and died as a result. At least he went out doing something he loved. At the typical Sunday afternoon gatherings, we ate food they ordered from a deli or pizzas or Chinese takeout. Nana and Pops had met at UC Berkeley and were definitely on the liberal end of the spectrum. They loved to talk politics, except when Bart was there, it became a taboo subject after several discussions turned into heated arguments with AJ in tears and Dad and Bart yelling at each other. Dad told me Bart wasn't so bad when he and AJ first got together, but over the years had gotten more and more conservative. When Obama was elected, he would say horrible things that everybody learned to ignore. He would often sit by himself and scroll through his phone chuckling while everyone else talked about movies or books or new restaurants, anything but politics.

When Jason, Elijah and I were little, we used to get along fine. But around the time I turned nine or ten,

Jason started being mean to me. My Latino cousins' comments were annoying but not mean-spirited, whereas Jason would say things like, "You smell funny," which I guess he meant differently than white people did. One day, Jason, Elijah, and I were playing croquet, and I did something that made Jason mad. "That was a nigger thing to do," he shouted. Everybody heard it. Dad jumped up and yelled at AJ, "What the hell?"

He rushed over and grabbed me by the hand. "We're leaving."

I was still in a daze about what had happened, and I don't think I got the full impact until I saw Dad's face, red and furious. I knew what Jason said was rude and unacceptable, but I was more frightened by Dad's anger than the slur. "It's okay, Dad."

"No, it's not okay," he said, fixing his gaze on Bart, who had positioned himself behind Jason with a hand on his shoulder. Jason's initial panic that he had screwed up changed to a sneer.

"Chill, man," said Bart. "You're making a big deal out of nothing. They're just kids."

"Nothing? How can you say it's nothing? It's a sickness that people still use that word, and it seems to be getting worse lately."

AJ now stood next to Dad. "Jason, tell Colton you're sorry."

"April, stay out of this," said Bart. AJ's real name was April, but he was the only one who called her that. I remember the angry look in his eyes, like everyone in the family hated him. He stood tall, one man against the world, as if it was up to him alone to defend his son. "Probably something Jason just heard at school."

Dad stepped forward, still holding my hand. "Just as likely he heard it at home."

"You calling me a racist?"

M jumped up and shouted, "Hey," loud enough to shut everyone up. "Everybody calm down." Her words carried the weight of being the oldest, and even Bart tended to steer clear of her. She was a couple of years older than my dad and always seemed strong and sure. She was a psychiatrist who mostly focused on kids and young adults. She loosened my hand from Dad's and motioned for AJ's two boys to follow her, taking us a distance from the crowd that had formed around Bart.

She spoke in a calm voice, but with authority. "It's not okay to call someone out because they look different. When I was little, other kids used to call me Big Foot because I was bigger than everybody else." The three of us chuckled, and she joined in. "Now that's one thing. All kids do it. But it's never okay to call someone a name because of the color of his or her skin. You got it?"

"Yes, Aunt M."

"Now, Jason, shake hands with Colton." We did what we were told while Bart stood at a distance with his arms crossed. Apparently, Dad wasn't satisfied. He entered the circle and nodded to M. "I appreciate what you're doing, but we're still leaving." He took my hand and pulled me away.

Dad marched toward the gate, dragging me along, and Papi caught up with us, putting a hand on my shoulder.

"I don't think Jason meant to be mean."

Dad gave Papi a dirty look. "That's where parenting comes in. Even when AJ tried..."

"Don't," said Papi. "Not in front of our son."

"Why does she stay with him?"

"Augie, please." And for Papi he would shut it down. I think that's why they've been together so long.

When we got to the car, Dad's hands were shaking and Papi took the keys. "I'd better drive," he said. He eased the car onto the Bay Bridge and toward the fog that awaited us like it did every time we returned to the city from a Sunday gathering in Oakland.

On the new, wide-open part of the bridge, traffic glided smoothly, just like the sailboats on either side. But as we got to the tunnel, brake lights lit up one right after another. We all groaned as if the traffic jam was created just for us.

"It wasn't the first time," I said matter-of-factly from the back seat. I don't know what made me say it because things were just getting calm again.

"What?" said Dad.

"Jason said stuff like that before."

Papi took one hand off the steering wheel and placed it on Dad's leg, pleading for calm. "You should always tell one of us," said Papi sweetly, "when something like that happens."

I thought a minute. "I don't want to be a tattletale."

Dad squirmed in his seat and then turned around to look at me. "That's not the same as...as telling on a friend who steals a piece of candy. When someone uses a racial slur, we need to know."

"What's that mean?"

"When someone says something bad about you because of the color of your skin."

"Am I ever going to meet my mother?" That was around the time I first started thinking about meeting her but hadn't voiced it yet.

Papi glanced at Dad with a here-we-go look. "Here's the deal, Colie. Your daddy and I wanted a child, but we needed a woman to carry you in her tummy for nine months, you know, like we talked about. The woman who carried you—"

"My mother," I corrected.

Dad sighed and let Papi take over. "Yes, technically, she's your mother. She wasn't at a point in her life where she was ready to take care of a child, but she was happy to help us."

"Why wasn't she ready?" I asked.

"She had dreams of being a singer," Dad said. "Still does."

"Can I find her on YouTube?"

"Not yet," Dad said. "Making it in the music business is really hard."

"Yeah," Papi added. "Like any career in the arts. Like being a writer for instance." Dad hadn't taken a leave of absence yet to pursue his writing and I knew Papi was worried about not having enough money if he did. They had talked a lot about it.

"What's her name?" I asked.

"Joy," Dad said. "We had an agreement, Papi and I

would be your only parents, so it wouldn't be confusing to you."

I turned quiet, thinking I should let it go. Dad twisted around to give my leg a reassuring squeeze. "Maybe it doesn't make sense to you, but Joy thought if she couldn't be around all the time, maybe it was better to stay out of the picture altogether."

"Who wants ice cream?" said Papi.

His suggestion was met with surprising silence from me and a ho-hum "Okay" from Dad.

Twelve

The weekend after we got back from Los Angeles, Dad announced we had been invited to a leapling birthday party near Santa Cruz.

"What? Who?" said Papi.

"What's a leapling?" I asked.

"A leapling is someone who is born on the twenty-ninth of February. The husband of a friend of AJ's was born on February 29, 1980. It's his fortieth, so they're having a big party."

I did the calculations. "But isn't it really like his tenth birthday?"

"Very good," said Papi. "Clever."

"I wonder what he does on the years when there's no twenty-ninth," I said.

"That's a long way to drive for a party of someone we don't know," said Papi.

"Yeah," said Dad, "but AJ really wants us to go. She's taking Jason and Elijah. I think Lio is going too."

Since the incident of Jason's slur a few years before, the Sunday gatherings had fallen off, but not solely because of the tension between Dad and Bart. Pops passed away and not long after, Nana got very sick and passed as well. She was like the glue that held everything together. I saw Jason at her funeral. But it wasn't really a time to hang out and we barely spoke. It's too bad because I liked Elijah and wanted to get to know him better. But when Jason was around, Elijah was always in his shadow. In any case Dad had promised AJ we would go to the party and it sounded fun because it was going to be outside and there would be a DJ.

"It's still the rainy season," said Papi. "An outside party might be tricky."

"The forecast for Saturday is unseasonably warm and no rain. AJ says all the signs are for a go-ahead except one," said Dad.

"What's the one?" asked Papi.

"Everyone is expecting that some kind of lockdown is coming due to the virus. When the host first planned the party, there were two deaths in California and less than fifteen cases. Now the number of cases has doubled, and infections are taking off in a few hotspots around the country and in other parts of the world. AJ says they've decided to go ahead with party especially since it might be the last hurrah before a stay-at-home order."

"At least outside is safer, isn't it?" said Papi.

"Let's hope so," said Dad. "Anyway, most of the people coming down with the virus seem to be older and have other health complications. We should be good."

It was dusk when we turned off the highway onto a gravel road surrounded by redwood trees. The evening was warm, so with the windows down, we heard the music before the house came into view. And then around a bend we saw a gathering of people in the driveway of a house under strings of lights going from tree to tree. There was another light that projected multicolored dots onto the trees above them and tables piled with food. It was a real party with about thirty people. It reminded me of the parties we used to have with Papi's family. As it turned out, the person celebrating a birthday was Alberto, and he was also Mexican, adding to my impression that Mexicans liked to throw a good party.

By the time we parked the car up the road and walked to the gathering, it was almost dark. The first person I saw when we entered the lighted area was Jason sitting by himself, glued to his phone. He reminded me of his father at the Sunday family gatherings we used to have in Oakland.

"Why don't you go say hi to your cousins?" said Papi. "We're going to look for AJ so she can introduce us to the hosts." He carried a bottle of wine we had brought as a gift.

I went over to Jason. "Hey, Jason."

He looked up, said, "Hey," and then went back to his phone.

"Where's Elijah?"

"No idea." Okay. Some things never change. Haters gonna hate. But why?

I spotted Uncle Lio talking to an Asian woman near the food tables, which gave me an excuse to get away from Jason's weird-ass vibe. Lio was Dad's younger brother, and I loved him a lot. He was funny and always showed an interest in what I was doing. Dad said Lio was suffering from Peter Pan syndrome since he lost his job managing a dental office, flitting from one new idea to another. He had married young but was divorced and had a daughter around my age, who I had only met once or twice. Dad had rolled his eyes when he heard Lio was now pursuing acting, but I thought it was perfect for him. He was good-looking, athletic, and super popular with the ladies. Maybe he could give me some pointers with Olivia. I walked toward him, and as soon as he saw me, he waved me over and gave me a big hug. "Hey, my man. Good to see you. Geez, you're almost as tall as me."

"Give me a year or two and I'll be looking down on you."

He laughed. "Oh, you think you're a big man now that you have a girlfriend."

"How did you know about that?"

"Dude, you know there are no secrets in this family." Well, except what happened in Mexico and why AJ got divorced and what was going on with Aunt M and why Lio rarely saw his daughter and a bunch of other stuff.

"I hope we can go to England this summer. Olivia's brother is coming to visit soon, but she can't come because of school."

"Olivia. Sweet!"

He turned to the Asian woman and introduced me as his super cool nephew. We shook hands and she smiled, but I felt like I was intruding. I told him I wanted to talk to him later and asked if he had seen Elijah. He pointed to a small group of people near the DJ's table. "Catch you later, man," he said. "I want to hear more about Olivia."

The DJ was a large muscular Black man in sunglasses.

He looked intense. I thought it would be cool to talk to him about some of the music Olivia turned me on to, but he didn't seem very approachable. He was playing Latin music, which I didn't know much about, but it had a danceable beat.

Elijah was with a little girl about six who looked like she was teaching him a salsa step. His face was wrinkled in concentration and his lips counted the beat. The girl shook her head and sighed.

"Are you dancing now, cuz?"

He stopped his feet and dropped his hands. "Hey, Cole." His faced turned red. He was always shy and embarrassed easily. "This is Gaby. It's her father's birthday."

"Oh, cool. So, this is your house?" I said to Gaby.

"Uh-huh. Do you know how to salsa?" said Gaby.

"Not my thing."

"My parents are good salsa dancers. They taught me a long time ago."

I chuckled. "Like when you were born?" Elijah gave me a funny look, like it was an asshole thing to say.

"I'll be seven soon." She wore a glittery party dress and sneakers with LED lights that blinked when she moved.

"I'm sorry. That was mean."

"No problem. I have to go talk to Lamar," said Gaby, sounding like the grownup hostess of the party. "He's the DJ and my friend," she said over her shoulder. She walked around the table and touched the DJ's arm. He smiled down at her. She certainly acted a lot older than six.

"You know, the DJ is blind," said Elijah.

"No way!"

"Yep. That's why he wears those glasses. He looks kind of scary, but he's really nice."

"So, what's up with Jason?"

"Nothing. Well, you know, the divorce thing. We're supposed to be with Mom on the weekends and last weekend he refused to go. Mom got really upset. This weekend he agreed to come to the party, but he wasn't happy about it."

I know a divorce must be hard and the thought of my dads splitting up gave me the willies. I don't know what I would do. But it was hard for me to have a lot of sympathy for Jason, and he really didn't have to be a jerk about it. I might think he was avoiding me because he hated my guts, but it looked like he was avoiding everyone.

"Do you think you could introduce me to the DJ?"

"Probably when he takes a break. I'll ask Gaby to do it. They're really tight. He stays at a house down the road sometimes."

A few minutes later, the DJ had his headphones down around his neck, and Gaby took me in hand. "This is Colton," said Gaby. "He looks kind of like you."

Lamar laughed. "You mean Black?"

"Yeah."

He reached his hand out, and we did sort of an awkward soul shake. He pulled me briefly to his chest. "How you doing, brother?" I had this immediate warm feeling about him.

"I never met a DJ before."

"You like music?"

"Love it. Do you know this group called Easy Life?"

"Oh, yeah. British, right?"

"My girlfriend in England turned me on to them."

"What?" His voice went into higher surprise range. "How old are you?"

"Fourteen."

"How the hell you got a girlfriend in England?"

"I met her when we were on vacation in Thailand."

"Damn. You got the life. I've never been out of the country." He dropped his hand to the soundboard and made a couple of adjustments. "Have you ever played around with a controller before? I could show you a few things of what I do if you're interested."

"That would be awesome!"

He took me around the table to his setup and explained a little about the controller. He put the headphones on me and then placed my hand on the different levers and showed how the sound changed when you moved them up and down. I looked up at the kitchen window and saw AJ and Dad watching us. AJ smiled and waved.

I took off the headphones. "That's so cool. Thank you."

"What song of Easy Life do you like?" asked Lamar.

"One called Sangria with Arlo Parks. It's kinda my girlfriend's and my song."

"Maybe I can pull it up and play it."

"Probably better not. My dads don't like me listening to it because of the language."

"Did you say dads, like plural?"

"Yeah, they're gay."

He grinned. "Most of the time when you have two dads

they're gay."

"I guess so."

He put his arm around me. "I like you. You are one straight up cool dude."

In my life, I hadn't spent much time around other Black people. Since I grew up in the Mission and my dads were white and Latino, I mostly had white and Latino friends. When I got to Mission High, I became friendly with a couple of Black guys on the basketball team, but still hung out with Fer and Josh and their friends. In the last few months, I had met Olivia, Devlin, Joanna, and now Lamar. And there was Joy, of course, but that still felt a little strange. It seemed like these people came into my life just at the right time. In the larger picture, everybody was talking about Black Lives Matter and Black awareness. It's not like I ever felt ashamed to be Black, but there sure were times I felt different, especially when other people pointed it out or made those strange comments like I mentioned before. As a kid, you don't think about your identity so much, but as my dads kept telling me, being a teenager is different in so many ways, not just your racial identity. It's like this whole new world of finding yourself.

When I first said I wanted to meet my mother, I thought it was more about the experience of having a mother, not that there was anything lacking in my life in terms of affection and nurturing. Joanna told me in the little conversation we had, that she saw my dads as super loving parents and I was lucky to have them. Then I started thinking I wanted to meet Joy because she was Black, and maybe that was what I needed in my life. More contact with people like me. That hadn't worked out so well with Joy. I couldn't wait until Devlin came for his visit and I could talk to him about some of this stuff.

I spent most of the party hanging out with Elijah and Gaby. She was a hoot and way beyond her age. She kept going up to people and telling them they should dance, at times physically pulling them out of their chairs and offering to teach them to salsa. At one point, she went over to Lamar to apologize for not being more successful in getting the crowd to dance and hugged him from the side. He leaned down and kissed the top of her head, showing the obvious affection between them. Something Gaby said to him seemed to give him an idea, and he stopped the music.

"This next song is dedicated to someone special out there." The song started with a whistling of the melody. He had it on a loop so it could play softly while he spoke. "I hope everyone here has someone special. I know at least one person out there who has a love far away." It gave me chills that he said that. We had just met, and yet he was throwing me a shoutout in a subtle way. "Okay, now, when we get to the chorus, I want everyone to sing 'To my love, to my love.' Sing it to your love. Dance for your love." Then he brought in the synth track, building, building, then percussion. The song was mostly in Spanish except for the chorus, and I later found out it was a Colombian group.

Everyone smiled and looked around. The music was hypnotic, making it hard not to move. The song came to the chorus, and Lamar shouted into the microphone, "To my love, to my love. TO MY LOVE." He stopped the song and played 'to my love' on a loop. "Come on, everybody." People joined in, a few at first, and then the forest echoed with everyone shouting, "To my love."

Gaby touched my arm, and I leaned down. She cupped her hand to my ear. "I think that song is for my Tio George."

"Who?" I asked. Elijah leaned in to hear what we were talking about.

"My uncle. Well, sort of my uncle. He lives in the little cottage next to our house." She pointed to an older man who stood at the edge of the crowd and looked uncomfortable.

"Him? Are you sure?" said Elijah.

Gaby looked at both of us like we were children and tsked. She put her arms akimbo. "I saw them kissing."

Not that I should be surprised that someone is gay, but I really did not see that coming: a big, muscular, Black, blind DJ, and he was gay. "I have two dads," I said. I wasn't sure she was old enough for such information, but she had a brilliant comeback.

"I've just got a regular mom and dad," she said, as if it was a disappointment. "But I might end up with two uncles if they... you know..."

All I could do was shake my head. I noticed Tio George looked upset, and then he disappeared into the darkness, away from the lights.

AJ came out of the kitchen with a big platter of vegetables. She put it down on the table and came over to say hi. She hugged me and asked if I had learned some DJ tricks. She looked a little concerned about something but was trying not to show it. "Have you seen your brother?" she asked Elijah.

"He was here, but when the song started, he said, 'This is bullshit,' and took off."

"What do you mean, took off?"

"He went behind the house."

AJ hurried in the direction where Elijah had pointed.

"She doesn't seem very happy," I said.

Elijah shrugged. "She didn't even say anything when I said 'bullshit.' His words, not mine."

Lamar stopped the music, and someone came out of the house with a big cake with lots of candles, the little flames fluttering in the wind. "That's my mom," said Gaby. Her father was talking to Papi and acted surprised when everyone started singing happy birthday. While the singing was still going on, AJ and George returned from the direction of George's house, looking even more upset. AJ scanned the crowd, and I assumed she hadn't found Jason. She came to us and asked Elijah again, "Have you seen Jason?"

"God, Mom, you keep asking me that. Am I supposed to keep track of him every minute?"

She looked upset with his tone of voice but checked herself. "No, honey. I'm sorry. I need to find him."

"All right. I'll help you look," said Elijah.

"I can help too," I said.

"Have some cake first. I don't want you guys to miss out."

After the cake and champagne, people started to leave.

AJ was talking to Lio and kept shaking her head and pointing in different directions. Gaby's mother hugged departing guests and looked very happy at how the party had gone. But when AJ approached her and they talked a minute, her face changed.

I noticed Lamar was packing up his equipment with George's help, and I walked over to thank him again for showing me some DJ techniques. I heard him say, "When I did shit like that, my mom let me suffer the consequences. She might've even called the cops herself."

George grabbed Lamar's bicep to get his attention. "Oh, your protégé is here."

It was awkward to come in on the middle of a conversation that I was sure was about Jason. "Sorry. I just wanted to thank you again."

"Ah, the cool dude," Lamar said with a big smile. "If you're ever in these parts again, I can show you more stuff. And we'll listen to that song you like when your parents aren't around." He chuckled.

"I'd like that," I said. "Looks like you're leaving, so I'll say goodbye."

"Give me a hug, man. Until next time."

A short time later, I saw Gaby's father, Alberto, organizing a search party for Jason. "I'll get some flashlights," said Rebecca, Gaby's mother.

"What's a birthday party without some drama?" said Alberto.

Everyone gathered on the driveway, and George returned from walking Lamar home. I had this image in my head of them kissing goodnight.

Alberto took charge. "We'll go into the woods in two groups, one led by me and one by George. Stay in your group. We don't need this to be the next creepy horror flick." He paused for laughter, though no one even broke a smile. "Everyone needs a flashlight or your cell phone light. In my group, Augie, Ruben, Colton, and Elijah. In George's group, Byron, Rafael, and Lio. Rebecca and AJ should stay here in case he comes back."

"Great. I can start cleaning the mess," said Rebecca, looking around at the half-eaten trays of food and the bottles and cans scattered about the area.

"I want to go," said Gaby.

"Absolutely not," Alberto said. "Help your mom clean up. George, your group should follow the trail out the back of your house over to the next road. My group will walk down our road until the next trail and then head into the woods. If he comes back, someone call us."

When we were in the woods, Dad asked me if I had talked to Jason at the party. "Do you know what's going on?"

"He wouldn't talk to me, but Elijah told me he refused to go to AJ's house last weekend. Elijah thinks he wants to stay with his dad full time."

"I'm glad you got to spend some time with Elijah, at least."

"The party was fun, and the DJ showed me some stuff. He's a really cool guy and I think he's gay."

"I heard. I'm glad you had a good time."

"I feel bad for AJ," said Papi. "Please, mijo, if you're ever feeling really bad like that, talk to us. If you disappeared like Jason did, it would kill Dad and me."

"I'm nothing like Jason."

"We know you're not," said Dad.

About an hour later, the search was called off. Jason had been picked up hitchhiking by the Santa Cruz police. AJ went to the station to get him and we started the long drive home.

Thirteen

One more secret was added to the family chest. In the next few days, I heard my dads talking about Jason several times, but as soon as I entered the room, they would change the subject. I had a sneaking suspicion that there was more to the story than disappearing from the party and getting picked up by the local cops, as if that wasn't bad enough. I did learn that his plan was to go back to his father's house in Modesto, which was a long way from Santa Cruz. What was he thinking? How was he planning to get there? Hitchhike all the way? But one time I was able to hear a little more of their conversation before my dads realized I was listening.

"Colton would never do that," said Papi.

"Well, there was that Target incident," said Dad.

Ah-hah. Sounds like something was stolen. From Gaby's house? Or George's? The plot thickens. I also remembered Lamar saying his mom might have him arrested if he had done something like that. Since I had spent a good part of my life around a lot of adults (one of the perks or disadvantages of being an only child, depending on how you looked at it) I felt like I was a pretty good at reading situations. I was determined to get to the bottom of what was going on with Jason. Maybe I would make a good spy.

But I didn't have much time to worry about Jason because Devlin was scheduled to arrive the following day, and I was super excited about it. Of course, I would have been a lot more excited if he was bringing Olivia with him, but it was sort of the next best thing. I liked both of them so much and didn't understand why they were constantly bickering and putting each other down. Again, being an only child, I had this feeling that if I had a brother or sister, I would be so happy I would never fight with them.

That day Olivia and I got caught kissing, I told her how lucky she was to have a brother and that being an only child wasn't much fun.

"That's what Mum says," said Olivia. "That I'll look back one day and realize how great it was to have a sibling. She was an only child, since her mum couldn't have any more children after her. I don't know. I suppose he's all right sometimes. But he can also be such a wanker."

"A what?"

She looked at me like I was crazy. "You're not aware of what wanker means?" She would occasionally have this attitude that Americans were from another and inferior planet like she did that day on the bicycle tour. It was the one thing about her that got under my skin.

"No. Should I?" I said innocently. The truth was that I had heard Devlin say it one day when Olivia wasn't around, and he told me what it meant, but I wanted to tease her a little bit by making her explain it to me.

"It's like an arsehole, or what you call a jerk."

"But doesn't it mean something else?"

Major eye roll. "I can't believe you don't know what a wank is?"

"Nope."

She was beginning to be suspicious about my ignorance and gave me a sideways down-the-nose look. "You're going to make me say it?"

"Uh-huh."

"Masturbate, you muppet."

"What's a muppet?" At that point, I couldn't control it any longer and burst out laughing.

"You've been pulling my leg all along. I'm done with you."

"I still think your brother is really awesome."

"You don't have to live with him."

So, I was getting my chance to live with him, at least for a couple of weeks. We had a two-bedroom house, and it was decided he would sleep in my room. I would give him the bed since he was the guest, and I would sleep on an air mattress on the floor.

A couple of days before he arrived, I noticed some tension between Dad and Papi, but I didn't believe it had anything to do with Devlin until I overheard Papi say, "You act like you're sixteen around him. You're not, Augie." At least he didn't say fourteen. That would have been a real insult. I began to wonder if Devlin was gay, this guy that was going to be sharing my room, not that I cared. I had met plenty of my dads' friends and now Lamar, who were all awesome gay people. It's just that it gets a little confusing when Devlin's parents had said something about a girlfriend. My dads have always been very open and willing to talk about issues of sexuality. But that still didn't make them completely understandable, especially when I heard so many crazy things that kids at school believed about sexuality. There was this one guy in one of my classes who said he was bisexual, but I wasn't sure how that worked. I wanted to talk to Devlin about it, but I had no idea how to begin that conversation.

That first night Devlin and I went to bed early because I had school the next day and he was jetlagged. I should have let him sleep, but I was crazy to talk about Olivia. I had thought up a bunch of covert questions to get information, like if she really liked me or if she was still seeing that old boyfriend. He saw through me in about two seconds. "Yes, she really likes you. And that other boyfriend is yesterday's news. When her girlfriends come over, she can't stop going on about you. Now, might I go to sleep? I'm knackered."

"One more thing. I want to start working out. Can you show me some things while you're here?"

"Do you have any equipment?"

"No."

"We'll improvise. I'm waking you up early, so we can get some exercise in before you go to school. No whinging, all right?"

I assumed he meant complaining, but I wasn't going to be a wanker and ask him what it meant. Speaking of wanking, I guess I was going to have to change my habits while he was there.

The next morning, he was up at the crack of dawn and

kicked the air mattress. Of course, I had lain awake long after he settled into the raspy breathing of sleep, thinking about my life and stuff. Now I was knackered. "Rise and shine, mate. Work out time."

"No," I moaned. "Can't we start tomorrow?"

"Livie was just telling me the other day how much she likes boys with muscles."

"That's not what she told me."

"She didn't want to make you feel bad about your skinny arms."

"They're not that skinny."

"Anyway, you work out for yourself. Not for other people."

"Yeah, right."

In the living room, he had everything set up: a chair from the dining room, some heavy books from the bookshelf, and a large bottle of detergent from the laundry room. With the dining chair, he showed me how to do tricep dips and incline and decline pushups. Then we did squats holding a big dictionary and bicep curls holding two large books. We used the detergent bottle like a kettlebell and lifted it over our heads.

Dad came to the door of the living room, holding a cup of coffee. "What's all this huffing and puffing?"

"Your son wants muscles," said Devlin. "Would you like to join us?"

"I can't think of anything more fun at this hour of the morning, but I tweaked my back recently."

"Liar," said Devlin.

"Look, Dad." I rolled up the sleeve of my T-shirt and

flexed my bicep. Devlin was wearing a tank top, and I noticed Dad staring at his biceps and ignoring mine. "Uh, Dad?" I said, trying to get his attention.

"Great, but it's time you hit the shower and got ready for school. I suppose you'll want a high protein breakfast," said Dad with a bored expression.

"I'd be happy to fix some eggs so you can rest your back," said Devlin.

"Very funny. But you don't have to."

"Seriously, I'm a wiz in the kitchen. Breakfast is my specialty."

"Have at it. I'll be in my writing cave."

While Devlin fixed breakfast, I sat at the counter and finished up some homework I should have done the night before. Dad didn't even get on my case because he knew how excited I was about having Devlin there. Papi came into the kitchen and asked, "Why is there a bottle of detergent in the living room?"

"Sorry, mate. We were having a workout."

I ran and got the bottle and then showed him how we used it to do over-the-head lifts. "Next time I see Olivia, she won't even recognize me."

Papi looked at my schoolbooks on the counter. "Does Dad know you didn't finish your homework?"

"I guess with all the excitement yesterday evening, he forgot to ask."

"Okay. Our secret. But don't make a habit of it."

Devlin turned to Papi. "I made some breakfast. Should I pour you some coffee?"

"No tea?"

"You want a cuppa?"

"Just kidding. Coffee's good. Thanks."

We fell into a pattern for school days. Devlin and I would do the morning workout and I would flex my muscles in front of the mirror before I took my shower, sure that I was making progress. Then Dev would walk me to school and head off for downtown or Golden Gate Park or North Beach. At night, we would all have dinner together. Dev was a good cook (far better, I soon realized, than my dads) and offered to prepare meals every night. He made a great lasagna one night, a bouillabaisse another. On Friday he made conch fritters, a dish his Bahamian grandmother had taught him.

On the first weekend, the four of us drove across the Golden Gate bridge and went ziplining at a place in Sonoma County at Devlin's suggestion. Dad was lukewarm about it, but Papi and I were really excited. The lines took us high above the redwoods, and the guide showed how we could make our bodies into a cannonball so we would go faster. Dev and I did that and screamed as loud as we could while zipping over the treetops.

Papi said he enjoyed it, but Dad looked like he had seen a ghost every time he arrived, twisted backwards at the next landing and had trouble getting his footing to stick it. The guide told Dad how to right himself if he got twisted, but he never figured it out. He was usually the last one of our group of ten to take off, but on the final run I told him he should be one of the earlier ones so there wouldn't be such a big crowd watching his awkward landing at the other end. Dad sighed and stepped in front of me at the take-off point. Since it was the longest zipline, the guide told us to get a good running start down the ramp to have the momentum to make it to the end. Dad got hooked onto the cable, the guide said "Clear" into his walkie-talkie, and Dad started down the ramp. Halfway down the ramp, he stumbled and almost fell to his knees and several people gasped. And the next thing he was bouncing in the air but instead of stretching his legs out in front of him, he decided to draw in his knees, I guess because he had caught his toe on the wood. The cannonball position caused him to go faster than ever. We heard this fading, "Whoa!" and Papi and I looked at each other with eyes wide open.

When we got to the other end, we asked Dad if he was okay. "It goes so fast you can't see a damn thing," he complained. "I came within inches of hitting the top of that one tree."

"No, Dad, you weren't that close. But I thought you said you couldn't see anything."

"One big blur."

We all had a good laugh, and I think even Dad appreciated sharing this experience as a family. He finally relaxed when we sat down to lunch at a local winery. Devlin was still a few months short of his twenty-first birthday, but they served him wine without carding him. He had grown a little mustache and a goatee since Thailand, which made him look older.

When we got home, nobody felt like cooking, so we ate the leftovers in the fridge from all the food Devlin had cooked in the last few days. They continued to drink wine they had bought at the winery that Papi said we couldn't afford, and Dev offered to contribute, but Dad said no and paid for it. They got silly and I kind of liked when they drank because Dad loosened up and would make stupid jokes. Then we started teasing Dad for being such a doofus on the zipline and he whined how he had always been a nerd and was the last one picked for teams at school.

"I wasn't athletic like all of you, so on top of everything else (I assume he meant being Jewish and gay) I got called all kinds of names." It almost looked like he was going to cry. At first, I thought he was faking it, but then I realized he had gone from joking to sad in two seconds, like genuinely sad. Dev realized it too, got up, and walked around the table to give Dad a big hug from behind his chair. It was spontaneous and sweet.

Papi got a scowl on his face. "What the hell are you doing?" he shouted. His eyes looked like he was having trouble focusing and his speech was thick. He stood up so fast the chair fell backwards, and he grabbed the edge of the table so he didn't fall with it. I had never seen him like that. It all had happened so fast. Dev released Dad and backed up. Everybody had a shocked look on his face.

"Ruben, what's the matter with you?" said Dad. "You're being ridiculous." He gestured in my direction, reminding Papi I was there like he didn't want me to observe what was going on. The look on Papi's face was heartbreaking: embarrassment, sadness, anger. He let go of the table, weaved out of the dining room to their bedroom, and slammed the door. "I'm sorry you had to witness that," said Dad. "We've all had too much to drink."

Dev let out a sigh of exasperation but followed Papi and we heard him knock on the door and apologize. And Papi must have opened the door because they were soon talking quietly, though we couldn't hear what they were saying. Dad asked me to help him clear the table, but we left everything in the sink because he said he was tired. We had finished cleaning off the table and put the remaining food in the fridge when Dev walked calmly back in the kitchen. He stood at the sink, turned on the water, and started washing the dishes until Dad said not to, that we could do it in the morning.

We had planned to watch a movie, but Dad said he was going to bed. He said Dev and I could rent whatever we wanted. We made popcorn, sat on the couch with our feet on the coffee table, huddled under a big blanket, and watched Mission Impossible: Fallout. About halfway through, Dev fell asleep. I watched the movie until the end. He looked so peaceful. I hated to wake him to go to bed. He opened his eyes, looking surprised to see me leaning over him. "Is everything okay?" I asked.

"Don't worry, mate. Everything's hunky-dory."

We slept in the next morning with no workout. I went into the kitchen and Papi was making coffee. He turned around and smiled. "Buenas dias, mijo."

I walked over to him and gave him a hug.

Devlin came in a minute later. "Morning," he said.

"I made some coffee," said Papi in a cheery voice. "Or would you like tea?"

"Coffee's good, mate."

Everything seemed right with the world, and I let out a big sigh of relief.

The next week things were back to normal: morning workouts, Dev spending the day wandering around the city after he dropped me off at school and then came home to cook wonderful dinners. Dad passed the day in his writing cave while Papi went to work.

The thing that wasn't normal was the news. The governor of California declared a state of emergency due to the pandemic and we saw a report about the cruise ship Aunt M and her husband were on. They had detected a number of Covid cases among the passengers and crew on the way back from Mexico, so they had to quarantine at an air force base before they could go home. People started talking about schools closing, which was exciting like the possibility of snow days that students in other parts of the country had, but we didn't. They said the closure would probably be for three weeks. If that happened, I wondered about basketball practice. I would miss that a lot more than being in class.

Papi was a manager at Costco, and they told him he could start working from home if he wanted. That meant both parents would be home all the time. Devlin's return flight to London was canceled, but he was able to get on one two days earlier to make sure he got home in time to begin his internship. I was sorry his visit was being cut short because I was getting used to having a big brother, and I swore I was making progress on the muscle front. It was great having him drop me off at school and everybody asking who that cool guy was. "I didn't know you had a brother," a few people said.

We had a going-away dinner at a restaurant in the Mission, and we made promises to get together in London in the summer, though health experts were already saying the virus might still be around and summer travel was dubious. The whole way to the airport to drop Dev off, I was fighting tears. He put his arm around my shoulders in the back seat.

"You'll carry on with the workout, right?" he said. "Next time I see you I want to see results."

"I promise."

"Text me about your progress."

"I will."

On the drive home, I felt the most down I had been in a long time. Dev was gone. I had no idea when I'd see Olivia again, and we were at the beginning of a pandemic, which could disrupt our lives for a while. No one had any idea how much and for how long.

Fourteen

The weekend after Dev left, my dads invited Elijah over to spend the night. I suppose they knew I was feeling lonely and thought the company would be good for me. I was cool with it since Elijah and I were starting to be friends. Dad told me that Jason was pretty much refusing to come to AJ's on the weekends and wanted to live full time with his dad, which made it easier for Elijah and me to hang out.

After my dads went to bed, Elijah and I stayed up talking. I asked him if Jason got in a lot of trouble for running away from the party, working my way to the topic if he had stolen something from one of the houses.

"Yeah, my dad thinks he was acting out because he feels uncomfortable with the weekends at Mom's," said Elijah. "My parents agreed it would be better for him to stay in Modesto and not go back and forth, which is what he wanted, anyway. My mom is pretty upset about it."

"So, how did he think he was going to get all the way to Modesto that night? That's a long way to hitchhike."

"He thought if he got to the bus station in Santa Cruz, he could take a bus."

"Did he have money for a ticket?"

"I don't know. Why?"

"I heard some money went missing from one of the houses at the party." I was just guessing here. No one had actually said that.

"I don't know anything about that. Are you accusing Jason of stealing money?"

"No. I heard some stuff. My dads were talking about what happened, but when I entered the room, they shut up. It just seems he was in trouble for something more than running away from the party."

"I know you don't like Jason, but you shouldn't accuse him of things you don't know anything about."

Elijah was loyal to his brother, always defended him. They were so different, I was surprised they got along. Since I never had a brother, I wasn't sure how relationships between brothers worked. "You're right. I'm sorry. Anyway, I never had anything against Jason. He was the one that was always giving me a hard time. Why do you think he's so upset with your mom?"

"He blames her for the divorce and always takes Dad's side. Plus, Dad drinks a lot and yaks to my grandma, who helps take care of us, so we hear stuff we probably shouldn't. One night, he started going on about Mom being in Mexico that time she stayed when the others came back. He said she had probably met a sleazy Mexican, and he started going on about what a horrible place it was down there, and she shouldn't be there. Then he got on this thing about illegals coming across the border and stealing all the jobs. Because we were in the same room, Grandma told him to shush. My dad is not fond of Mexicans, obviously." Or Blacks or gays or anybody different.

"Do you think there's any truth in that? The part about meeting a Mexican?"

"I don't know for sure. My parents were always arguing even before the Mexico trip. Mom is a lot happier on her own. A couple of times, I've heard her chatting online with someone on the computer. The guy sounds like he has an accent."

"I'm going to tell you something, but you have to promise not to tell anyone I told you. I was supposed to keep it a secret. When my dads and I came back from President's Day week in Los Angeles, we ran into your mom at the airport. At first, she didn't want to say where she had been, but Dad managed to get it out of her. She had been in Mexico."

Elijah looked surprised, then a little scared, and finally, like something clicked in his brain. "Yeah, I remember that weekend. She had Dad drop us off instead of coming to get us. That was the first time Jason refused to go to Oakland and Mom was really upset about it."

"Whatever you do, don't tell Jason. Things are bad enough already."

Elijah stared at the ceiling, all caught up in his thoughts like things were bumping around inside his head, and I felt bad for telling him. "Hey, how are things going at school?" I asked.

"I think I'm going to high school in Oakland or Berkeley in the fall. I'm pretty sure I'm going to live with Mom full time. I want to go to Berkeley High if I can get in."

"That would be cool. Did you hear they might be closing schools for a few weeks because of the pandemic?"

"Mom says I can stay with her all the time if that happens. Going back and forth isn't much fun."

The following week, schools closed as expected and everyone was supposed to stay home. School districts started moving to online classes. People wore masks in the street. Restaurants, movie theaters, and playgrounds were closed. Olivia said the same thing was happening in England. Both my dads were home all the time now, and we got an announcement that classes would begin online soon. At first, it was total chaos. Nobody was prepared. A lot of students blew off classes because they thought they could get away with it and others because they didn't have computers at home. Some students would sign in and then disappear.

Since very few positive cases were among young people, my dads let me hang out with Fer, but we couldn't go into each other's houses. We tried to go to the playground to shoot some hoops, but the gates were locked, and a big sign said it was closed until further notice. Fer and I started playing games remotely online.

One night, Dad and Papi sat me down in the living room with their eyes narrowed and lines on their foreheads. Uh-oh, I thought. What did I do now?

"Am I in trouble?" I asked.

"No," said Dad. "It's nothing you did. We wanted to tell you about something that's going on with your Aunt M."

"Did she get covid or something from that cruise ship they were on?"

"Thank God, no. Remember that conversation we had a while back about girls who felt like boys inside and vice versa?"

"Yeah."

"Well, M has decided she's not really a woman inside and she's starting therapy to make some changes so she can feel and look more like the person she is inside."

"Oh," I said. "So, she's transgender. There are a few kids at school like that. It's sad they don't get treated very well. People are mean to them." Papi squirmed in his chair and he had an awkward smile on his face. I could tell he probably would have preferred they not tell me this news. His general attitude was that the less I knew about certain things, the better. But it was Dad's sister (soon to be brother), so I imagine he let Dad make the decision.

Of Dad's siblings, I knew M the least. She had been married to Arnie for a long time, but they had no kids. They were always nice to me though they were generally serious in family gatherings, preferring to talk about books, politics, movies, and travel. She was a psychiatrist, and he was a medical doctor. M was very athletic and played a lot of golf and tennis. I guess it's okay to say she was kind of masculine. She always cut her hair short and never wore a dress. She had a commanding voice and often took charge of things as the oldest sibling.

"We wanted to tell you because you will probably start noticing physical changes in the next few months, though who knows when we'll see her next with the pandemic. She's already begun therapy."

"What kind of therapy?"

"She takes testosterone injections. It causes things like facial hair growth, increased muscle mass, and a deeper voice, so her outside can reflect how she feels inside." I wanted to ask where I could get some of that stuff, but I knew it wouldn't be received well. I kind of chuckled inside, anyway.

"What about pronouns? I know some people use they/them." I wasn't a total troglodyte (that word again).

"Good of you to ask. She wants us to start using he/him. So, I guess I should say, he wants us to use he/him."

"What about Arnie?" I asked.

"I'm not going to get into that. That's personal between them. I know it will be... is hard for him."

"Does everybody know about M? Is it okay to talk about it?"

"Family and friends know. Soon I think everybody will know. It's probably okay if you talk to Olivia and Devlin about it as long as you do it respectfully."

"Of course."

"He will soon tell all his patients and probably reduce his practice, at least at first. I think he's going to switch to doing gender identity counseling. Do you have any other questions?"

"I think I'll do some research online. I'd like to know more about what M's going through."

Dad gave me this adoring look and Papi nodded his head with a little grin. I was so glad I didn't make a joke about wanting testosterone. I already had hair on my legs and crotch, but I sometimes felt like I wasn't masculine enough.

That night, I was getting ready for bed and listening to Khai Dreams with my headphones on. Dad came to the door and motioned for me to take them off. He sat on my bed.

"I'm so proud of you at the way you handled the news about M. A parent has a lot of dreams for their kids, probably too many, but what I realized today is that my hope you'd be a compassionate person came true. You showed compassion and intelligence in your comments and questions. I love you so much."

"Gosh, Dad, you're going to get me all emotional and that's not good right before you go to bed."

Dad shook his head. "And sometimes you're a wiseass."

"Sorry. I love you too. And you know, I didn't get this way by accident. You and Papi might have had a little to do with it."

"Papi and I really had no idea what we were doing when we had you. We just knew we wanted to do it."

"Do you think most people know what they're doing when they have kids? They don't exactly teach it in school."

"You're right."

"Can you tell me the story of my birth again? What went down? I love that story."

"Oh, honey, I've told that story so many times."

"But it's been a really long time."

His eyes lit up, and he got comfortable on my bed, kicking off his shoes and stretching out with his head against the headboard. "As you know, I can't stand the sight of blood, so I declined to be in the delivery room for your birth. All our friends and family pressured me to be present at that wondrous moment when my son entered the world. The decision was excruciating, but the fear of passing out and embarrassing everyone vanquished the other considerations. I knew I wouldn't love you any less by not being witness to your beautiful little head emerging from... uh... down there. I hoped you wouldn't resent me for not being there."

"Of course not, Dad."

"Papi, on the other hand, couldn't wait to participate. He had spent some time in Los Angeles, going to birthing classes with Joy, and had read a hundred books on the subject. They had been friends since college and had that special connection of having played in a band together. He played bass, and she was the singer. He wouldn't miss the chance of this new composition, holding her hand and telling her to push."

"How come we don't have any recordings of that band? I'd love to hear what they sounded like."

"You know the story. The guitar player, who had all the tapes, was mentally unstable. He was so angry when the band split up, he destroyed all the tapes."

"What a waste!"

"Anyway, I paced the waiting room, thinking I was a fool. Why couldn't I have just tamped down my fears and been present at my son's birth? Could it be worse than this waiting, not knowing? The seconds ticked on the large wall clock. The TV high on the wall was tuned to CNN, a constant loop of the doom and gloom of the housing crisis, banks failing, people losing everything.

It seemed a completely inappropriate background for this extraordinary event. I was obsessed with finding the remote so I could change the channel to something like a nature channel and went all around the room looking for it. I was kind of like you when we hide the remote to keep you from fiddling with it all the time."

"Come on, Dad. Get to the good part," I said. "No going off on tangents."

"You wanted me to tell the story. I'm telling it my way. I started down the hall to look for an aide who might be able to change the channel. Halfway to the nurses' station, I ran into Papi on his way to get me. By the beautiful expression on his face, I could tell things had gone well. He said it was an amazing experience, and you and Joy were resting. Everyone involved in the process said you should have a little time with her. Now that the messy part was over, I was hell-bent on getting to the room. I took Papi by the arm and said, 'Let's go in.' But you know your Papi. He told me not to be selfish and to give you two a minute because he had read you needed to confirm the smells you'd become used to over the nine months."

"That sounds strange, but whatever."

"He pulled me into a hug and calmed me down. Your Papi is such a good man. We held each other so tight I could feel his heart beat against mine like they were beating at the same rhythm. Thump. Thump. Thump."

"I love that part."

"We stood in the middle of the hallway oblivious to the people hurrying by, holding on to each other, strengthening each other for the moment we would meet you, our son, as a team. It was hard to believe two years of endless waiting were coming to an end. Papi and I entered the room. The lights were soft. And there you were. Our son. I had no idea how I was going to feel, but I hadn't quite imagined the intense, overpowering love I felt. Joy was gazing down at you, barely seeming to notice the other people in the room. I have to say it was a beautiful sight. Mother and child."

"That part makes me a little sad."

"I know. But we had an agreement, and the moment had arrived for you to go from her arms to ours. The nurse took the baby, and Joy lay back and closed her eyes. The nurse motioned for us to follow her. In an adjoining room, the nurse said she was going to do a little cleanup and examination, and that we could watch."

"So, was I all covered with blood and stuff?"

Dad got a dizzy look, like he was going to pass out. "Oh my God, no. I mean... we're not going to talk about that. She laid you down on the warming table and opened up the blanket. You punched and kicked with your tiny arms and legs. Your skin was purplish, especially your hands and feet. The nurse began to clean you with a large warm towel. I think you had pooped or something."

"Ew, gross, Dad."

"The nurse said it was a good sign." He laughed. "Then she moved her hands over your skin, behind the ears, the throat, the chest, the tummy. She turned you over and ran her fingers down your spine. When she gently rolled you over so you were again on your back, I asked if everything was okay. Papi told me to stop breathing down her neck."

"I can imagine you being all nervous and intense."

Dad shrugged. "That's the way I am. She said you were perfect, of course. She weighed you, took your vitals, and made prints of your adorable little hands and feet. Ten fingers and ten toes."

"But what if I'd had nine fingers and seven toes?" Every time he told the story, I changed the number of fingers and toes.

"Of course, we would have loved you just the same. But parents always hope their kids don't have any physical traits that might make life more difficult."

"Like having black skin?" I blurted out.

Dad made a sound that was somewhere between a gasp and a gulp. "You... you're going off script."

"I know. That wasn't fair. But you could have found a white or Latino surrogate mom, right?"

"Joy was willing and available. We thought it better to go with someone we knew than a stranger. Your black skin is beautiful, and never let anyone tell you it's not. You are a wonderful, unique person and being Black is part of that. Okay, I'm going to be perfectly honest. Fifteen years ago, Papi and I were a little naïve in thinking that by the time you became a teenager, racism would have vanished like the dinosaurs. I'm sorry there are still people who..."

"...are troglodytes?"

"Exactly! But there are millions and millions and millions of people who will see you for the incredible person you are without thinking about the color of your skin.

And I suppose a few who find it particularly attractive, like maybe Olivia?" He danced his eyebrows up and down.

"She told me that the boyfriend she had before was white, but she felt more comfortable with me, like we could relate on a different level. Now, back to the story. My bad for getting into that heavy part."

"The nurse then wrapped our little bundle of joy in a blanket. She turned to us and told us it was time to take off our shirts. That morning, we had scrubbed our bodies in the shower. We had been told not to use deodorant. The idea is that we would have skin to skin contact with you to begin the bonding process. We stretched out on the two side-by-side lounge chairs that had been brought into the room. I felt self-conscious about my hairy chest. How would you react? Would it tickle you? Would it feel strange? When I'm nervous, I sweat, and since we couldn't wear deodorant, I was afraid you would be forever imprinted with the notion of a stinky, hairy dad."

"Yep. That's the first thing I think of when I think of my dad: hairy and stinky." We were stretched out, side by side on my narrow bed. I sniffed and waved my hand in front of my nose, giggling.

"Hey, watch it, buddy, or I'll stop before I get to the really good part." He crossed his arms and made a zipping motion over his lips.

"Please finish the story," I pleaded.

He shook his head, and I pleaded some more.

"All right. The nurse asked who wanted to go first. I looked at Papi and said he should go first. And he said, 'No, you.' We went back and forth like that while the nurse stood there and rolled her eyes. Papi looked at me with his sweet brown eyes and said, 'No, Augie, it has to be you.'"

Dad choked up at this last part and got tears in his eyes like he always did. "Did you start crying then?"

"I might have had a few tears in my eyes."

"Come on. You were crying like a baby."

"She put you on my chest, opening up the blanket so we would have skin-on-skin contact. I was at that moment and forever, a father. I thought my heart might burst. Papi said, 'Look at all that hair,' and he touched your head, choking on his words, half-laughing, half-crying. 'He looks just like you, Augie.' Okay, I admit it. I kind of lost it at that point. I shook with weeping. Now your first impression of me would be a hairy, stinky, hysterical dad. I passed you to Papi, afraid I might scare you. 'Here, Colton, meet your Papi.' That first time I said your name was magical, the two syllables that would become a song in my mouth for years to come—a love song, a sad country song, a hectic heavy metal song, a back-and-forth rap song, a silly pop song, but always a song."

Like every time he told the story, tears rolled down his cheeks. And every time I heard the story was a reminder that I had been born in unusual circumstances, but I was surrounded by a special kind of love.

Fifteen

The Black Lives Matter movement had been around a good part of my life, and I was vaguely aware of the police and vigilante murders of Black people, who almost certainly wouldn't have been killed if they had been white people in the same situation. Trayvon Martin was just a few years older than me, and Tamir Rice was only twelve. In the last few years there had been a ton of examples that made the news. I know my dads were torn between talking to me about those incidents and scaring the you-know-what out of me but possibly saving my life by making me aware, and not talking about them, being in denial in hopes that living in the Bay Area provided some security from such tragedies.

But after the Target incident and my best friend throwing me under the bus, something was beginning to happen inside me. I guess you could call it an awareness that it was much more likely something bad could happen to me than Josh or even Fer. Of course, it wasn't fair, though I didn't plan to sit around and whine about it. But once you have that realization, you can't just forget about it. It lives with you.

On the positive side, I had met Olivia, Devlin, and Joanna, making me proud to be Black. And yet the murders continued into 2020, Breonna Taylor, Ahmaud Arbery, and probably others I didn't hear about. I still didn't want to think about it much, preferring to play video games and basketball, chat with Olivia on WhatsApp, and discover new music. But when the news of George Floyd hit the streets and the video of the policemen with his knee on Floyd's neck circulated widely, something exploded in my head as well as in the conscience of a lot of Americans. My dads had begged me not to watch the video, but it was available everywhere. I went online and did a lot of research about BLM and all the injustice that led to it. At school, we were still struggling with the online format, but my history teacher tried to get a discussion started about the connection between racism and the BLM movement. Most of my classmates didn't have much to say, but I did, and I think I impressed the teacher with my knowledge of the subject.

Protests were happening all over the country and I wanted to attend one. My dads discouraged it, fearing violence and white supremacist backlash that could happen even in the Bay Area. They suggested finding other ways we could support BLM like a sign in the window.

"Sure, a sign in the window is great," I said. "But we need to do more. We need to be in the streets." They looked at me with both pride and fear.

Just like the thing with meeting my mom, I wouldn't let it go. After a while, they relented. Once we decided to go to a protest, Dad said he wanted to go to the protest in Oakland since it was his hometown and the fact that

Oakland had always been a center of Black pride. He even guilt-tripped his siblings into joining us, including M who was in the middle of his transition, and, at first, said no way. Elijah called and told me he had insisted that his mom let him go. We all agreed to wear masks and to try to maintain a distance from anyone who wasn't because, on top of everything else, there was still a pandemic going on. We also planned to go home before dark to avoid any chance of violence.

No one had seen M in person since he began his hormone therapy and we reminded each other that we had to use male pronouns, especially since we had arranged to pick him up at his house and drive to the Fox Theater where we would meet AJ, Lio, and Elijah under the marquee. Then we would all walk over to Frank Ogawa Plaza, where the rally would happen before the march.

M wore a baseball cap over his short haircut he said he had cut himself since salons and barbershops were closed. He wore a baggy sweatshirt and jeans. Dad had warned us we might notice a change in the timber of his voice since the last time we talked to him. In addition to the therapy, he was also taking online voice modulation classes. He seemed happy, but it was always difficult to tell with M. No one brought up the topic of Arnie.

As we got closer to the plaza, people streamed in from all directions, and angry shouts could be heard from the speakers. I held a sign that read, "If you think your mask makes it hard to breathe, imagine being Black in America." I had originally made one that said, "I don't want to be a statistic." My dads choked up after seeing it and told me they appreciated my anger but asked me if I would consider making a different sign.

When the march started down Broadway, we tried to stay at the edge of the crowd. AJ remained close to Elijah, and Dad kept telling me not to run ahead in my excitement. I was so thrilled to be doing something and felt proud to be there with my family. M marched alongside Lio, asking about his workout routine, which reminded me I hadn't kept up with the morning routine that Devlin set up for me. But I couldn't worry about that because the atmosphere of the march was amazing. There was a lot of righteous anger, but the marchers were peaceful. Almost everyone wore masks.

I worked hard to curb my urge to rush ahead and marched next to Elijah and AJ. At one point, AJ took out her phone, looked at it, and then put it back in her pocket. A minute later, it happened again. The third time she held it up to Elijah and said, "What does the caller ID say? I didn't bring my glasses."

"It says Highland Hospital." Highland Hospital was in Oakland.

"That's weird," she said. "I don't know anyone there and that's not our health plan." But she had a worried look on her face. It rang a fourth time, and she answered. She moved off to the side of the march and plugged her left ear against the noise. Lio and M stopped to wait and yelled at Elijah and me to slow down.

AJ leaned against a building and then slid down the wall to the ground. "What?" she shouted. "I can't hear you." Lio, Elijah, and I ran over to her.

"What is it?" said Lio.

AJ had a wild, confused look in her eyes. Her head shook no. She handed the phone to Lio. "There's a mistake. I can't understand what they're saying."

"Who are you trying to reach?" Lio shouted into the phone. Then he answered with a series of yeses to questions from the other end. "I'm Lio Burd. April's brother."

AJ stood up quickly. "Give me the phone," she screamed. "Is it Jason?" She tried to grab it out of Lio's hand, but he held her off.

Elijah and I looked at each other. "Jason's in Modesto, right?" I said.

Elijah nodded his head.

"I understand," Lio said and hung up. "We have to go to the hospital. There's been an accident. Bart and Jason. They couldn't give me any details."

AJ gawked at her brother like she couldn't decipher the words. She blinked and breathed in short, shallow gulps. "That's ridiculous. They're in Modesto."

"Colton," said Lio. "Run and get your dads and M. Tell them to come back here." Ironically, my dads had been the ones to get ahead of the rest of us and it seemed M had caught up to them.

"No, Colton," said AJ. "Don't go. You'll get lost. The people on the phone are wrong. We'll catch up with them. This is some kind of prank." She really didn't make sense.

"Go, Colton," said Lio in a voice that sounded angry.

"Oh my God, Lio, you're making a big deal out of nothing. There's obviously some kind of mistake." Her lips quivered and her face was losing its color.

Lio grabbed her arm. "AJ, listen to me. We have to go to the hospital right now. Something has happened." He turned to me but spoke calmly this time. "Cole, please go find your dads and M."

I found them only half a block ahead. They had turned around and were looking for us. When they saw me, they hurried toward me. "Where is everybody? I thought we agreed to stay together."

"AJ got a phone call from a hospital. Something happened to Jason and Bart."

"In Modesto?" said M.

"The call was from Highland here in Oakland."

We rushed back to others. AJ now stood like a statue, staring off into space.

"AJ and I have to go to Highland Hospital," Lio said. "Bart and Jason have been in an accident. Can you guys take Elijah?"

AJ kept shaking her head. "No, no, no," she said in a robotic voice. "This is a mistake."

"I'm going with you," said M. "You might need me."

M and Lio got on either side of AJ and led her toward the car. "What's happening? Elijah? Where's Elijah?" she mumbled.

"He's fine," said M. "He's with Augie and Ruben."

After they left, Elijah said, "I should have gone with them. It's my dad and brother."

"It's better to stay with us," said Dad. "Nobody can go into hospitals now, anyway. We'll walk back to the car and drive you over."

The marchers had all moved on, but we could hear

drumming and their shouts in the distance. "I hope it's not serious," I said to Elijah. It felt like a stupid thing to say. What do you say at a time like this? Part of me wanted to run and catch up with the march, but we were in the middle of a family crisis. I began to think about the worst-case scenario. Lio said it was an accident. What if...?

As we walked to the car, Elijah kept running ahead, trying to hurry us along. "Come on," he said. "We've got to get to the hospital."

Dad's phone rang, and he had a brief conversation in a low voice. Elijah saw him talking and ran back to us. "What's going on?" he said. "Are they okay?"

Dad had a very expressive face, and I knew all of its messages without his saying a word. This was not good. He tried really hard to sound even. "They say it's best not to go to the hospital. Um... like I said before, they don't allow visitors. We're all going to meet up later at AJ's house. Would you guys like something to eat?"

"No," said Elijah. He was angry, and I didn't blame him. Dad was obviously keeping something from us. "I want to go to the hospital. I need to be with my family."

"M and Lio are going to bring your mom home in a little bit. There's no point in going to the hospital."

"It's serious, isn't it?" said Elijah.

Dad hesitated, and I imagined all kinds of lies going through his head. But he simply said, "Yes."

"I knew it." Elijah wasn't angry anymore. He was scared.

As soon as we got to AJ's, Elijah asked, "Where's Mom?"

"She's sleeping," said M. "It's been a difficult day. I gave her something to sleep, so I think it's better if we don't disturb her."

Every few minutes, Elijah seemed to fall deeper into a slump. "Can someone please tell me what's going on?" He barely got the words out of his mouth.

"The last thing your mom said before drifting off to sleep was that she wanted us to tell you what happened," M said. We had all taken off our masks, and it was a terrible time to focus on this, but I couldn't stop looking at the hairs on his chin. His voice was definitely different, and he spoke deliberately and slowly to stay in control of it.

Lio took over and asked us all to sit down. Normally, the task would have fallen to M as the unofficial head of the family, but under the circumstances, or maybe at M's request, Lio took over. "Augie, could you get everyone some water?"

It's strange the things you remember from these momentous occasions. It was late afternoon, and the sun streamed in, focusing directly on a photo of the family on the mantelpiece: AJ, Bart, Jason, and Elijah. It was probably taken about three years before. Were they a happy family once?

Dad brought water bottles for everyone.

Lio took a deep breath. "Elijah, I'm very sad to tell you that your brother has died in the accident." The silence in the room was something you could almost reach out and touch. We all had stunned looks on our faces, but Elijah stared at the floor. It was like it hadn't hit him yet. "And Dad?" he said in a tiny voice.

"He's pretty banged up, but he'll be okay. He's in the

hospital."

"I don't get it," said Elijah. "Why were they in Oakland?"

Lio looked at M, and M nodded. "We weren't sure if we should tell you this," Lio began, "but you'll probably find out, anyway. It will be on the news. We think it's better you hear it from us. Your father was involved with the group..."

"I know. The Proud Boys. I talked to Mom about it."

"He and Jason were in a caravan of Proud Boys on the way to counter protest at the march we went to."

I sat up and my body jerked forward with anger. My own cousin and uncle were going to protest against me. Dad put his hand on my leg and his eyes were closed, as if begging me not to say anything. Everyone was staring at me. I sat back. This wasn't about me.

Lio continued. "It was an accident. The Proud Boys were bothering some people with Black Lives Matter bumper stickers. There happened to be a reporter in a news van that saw the whole thing. She had come to the hospital to get her report, and M got the whole story from her. It seems Bart was distracted and swerved into another lane to avoid hitting someone, but a car hit him from behind."

"So, it was his fault," said Elijah.

"It was an accident. I'm sure your father feels horrible. It's just a terrible, terrible accident."

I had a lot of things I wanted to say, but it wasn't the time. I couldn't imagine how Elijah felt, knowing that his brother died because his father put him in a dangerous situation. This was the kind of thing that can make your life go haywire. Elijah was going to need a lot of support. And then I thought of AJ upstairs in bed. She must have felt ten times worse. A mother losing her son. That's got to be the worst.

Sixteen

The ceremony in the chapel of the funeral home was small because we had to comply with a statewide mandate against gatherings of more than ten people. It was immediate family: AJ, Elijah, M, Lio, my dads and me. We all noted that M showed up without Arnie. Lio had sent an email to invite the Modesto grandparents without consulting AJ. Her siblings agreed it had to be done. As expected, they declined and sent a large floral bouquet. Bart was still recuperating in bed, and an investigation loomed over his head.

At dinner the night before the funeral, I asked my dads if Bart could be charged with something.

"I suppose they might go for involuntary manslaughter or, at least, criminal negligence," said Dad.

I had no sympathy for Bart since he was on his way to protest against Black folks trying to stop the killing of innocent people, but I was curious how he could be charged. "What exactly did he do that was against the law?"

"For one thing, he was part of a Proud Boys caravan that was harassing a couple of women in a car with Black Lives Matter bumper stickers," said Papi.

"I read online that the Proud Boys claim they aren't racists."

"That's the image they may try to project to protect themselves, but everybody knows they've got white supremacists in their ranks," said Dad. "There's another thing..."

"I don't think..." said Papi.

"It's going to be all over the news. He'll hear it, anyway."

"What?" I said.

"Bart and Jason had an assault rifle in the car, which is pretty much illegal in California."

"What?" I screamed. "They were going to shoot people at the march?"

"You know I'm not fond of Bart, but I find it hard to believe he had gone so far off the rails he would do something like that."

"I agree," said Papi. "He's probably like those guys in open-carry states that go to the supermarket with assault rifles strapped to their backs because they think it looks cool."

"Do you think Jason knew about the rifle?" I asked.

"Nah," said Dad. "I doubt it." I later learned that was a lie, but I understand why Dad didn't want me to know. Not only did Jason know about the rifle, but he was holding it in the air to show off to the women in the car they were harassing. That's what caused Bart to be distracted and lose control of the truck.

The ceremony was not religious, presided over by a friend of Nana and Pops who had grown up down the street from the family home in Oakland. It was short.

Lio, as the uncle closest to Jason, said a few words. Elijah surprised everyone by announcing he wanted to read a poem he had written. Poor guy. His voice started nervous and cracking but grew stronger.

"My brother fearless
Always the first on the rope swing
Yelled the loudest when he hit the lake
Stopped the guy trying to steal my bike
Even a noise in the dark didn't make him shake
My brother cool
Rode his skateboard wearing his shades
And his Jason and the Argonauts shirt
One day in his red kicks everyone liked
He picked up a snake in the dirt
My brother generous
Our Granny gave us two cookies
I dropped mine in the sand
At first he laughed but gave me half
When I needed help he gave me a hand
My brother sad
One day I caught him crying
He wouldn't tell me why
He made me promise not to tell
Cause if I did I'd die.
P.S. He didn't mean it

The poem made me realize how much he loved his brother. I wondered if he knew about the assault rifle and how everything went down. I hoped he didn't. Everyone was stunned. The pain had sucked all the air out of the room, leaving only the sound of AJ sobbing. Elijah looked at his mom with horror in his eyes in fear he had screwed up. Dad stood up and started clapping. One by one each of us rose and clapped and a lot of people were crying. I pulled down my mask, stuck two fingers in my mouth, and made a shrieking whistle I was famous for. It was spontaneous and kind of stupid, but I wanted so badly to support my cousin.

I had gotten everyone's attention and felt the spotlight on me. Now what did I do? I hadn't planned on saying anything, but I found myself walking to the front of the room. I met Elijah stepping down from the lectern, gave him a hug, and took his place in front of the group. Dad and Papi, knowing that I was still furious with Jason, looked at each other in fear of what might come out of my mouth. I had no idea what I was going to say, but I knew it wasn't a time for bitterness.

"I want to say I'm sorry, not just about the whistle, but about everything. I think everybody knows Jason and I weren't the best of friends; actually, we didn't get along at all. But he was my cousin, part of this family. The last time I saw him at a party, I knew he wasn't having a good time. I guess he felt out of place. I know what that's like. Maybe I could have done something. I could have introduced him to the DJ who was this really cool guy. Maybe the DJ could have showed him some stuff like he did me, you know, how to use the controls to fade and mix and stuff. It might have made him feel included. But I was selfish. My dads always taught me to try and help people who are in need." I stopped and sniffled. I was feeling pretty emotional. "But I did nothing. Jason was in need of a friend that day and I didn't help him. I'm sorry he's gone because that means we can't ever be friends. I can't tell him I'm sorry we didn't get along better."

The tears on people's faces had barely dried from Elijah's poem before they flowed again. Dad looked at me with a little smile and nodded. Papi wiped tears from his eyes. I knew they were proud of me, and, frankly, I was proud of myself. There's a place for anger, but there are some situations that call for you to be forgiving. I didn't understand why Jason followed so closely in his father's footsteps and why he was so desperate for his approval. Ultimately, the blame fell on Bart, and I believe the tragedy wouldn't have happened if Bart had been a better parent. Because the adults had all given up on Bart a long time ago, they had also given up on Jason, except for AJ, of course. I couldn't imagine what it was like for AJ to see her son going down the wrong path and not be able to stop it. Seeing how easily Jason had disappeared from our lives made me better understand why my dads were so protective of me and always on my case to be better.

After the ceremony, we all piled in our cars to drive to M's house, where we would gather on the patio and have something to eat. M had ordered Chinese food from everyone's favorite Little Shin Shin and had it delivered. He served Elijah and me lemonade made from the Meyer lemons in the yard. "The lemons just keep coming. I don't have to do anything. The rest of the yard is a mess," said M. Arnie was the gardener and had moved out.

For the adults, M opened bottles of wine. "I never know

what wine goes best with Chinese food," he said.

"The wine that gets you drunkest," said Lio. "Actually, do you have any vodka?"

"Will scotch do?" Arnie walked through the gate, holding a large bottle in a brown paper bag.

"Arnie, good to see you," said Dad. Pandemic etiquette took away the awkwardness of whether to hug or not. Dad moved close to Arnie, and they bumped elbows, the new acceptable greeting. Arnie made the rounds, touching elbows and put the bottle of scotch in Lio's hand. He got to M. Everyone tried to not stare at how M and Arnie would interact, but that was the focus of attention of the moment, like not being able to take your eyes away from a wreck on the side of the road. It was hard to imagine how a couple having problems would handle it when they had been married for a long time, but when one of them decided to change gender...? Because things were awkward, I asked Elijah if he wanted to set up croquet on the lawn.

"Yeah," said Elijah. "I'm not very hungry."

"Me, neither," I said. "We can eat later."

We set up the hoops and started playing. At my first strike with the mallet, I kicked up a clump of dried grass and dirt. "Oops!" I had never seen the grass so brown and dry, another indication that M had let things go.

At one point, Elijah hit a ball outside the boundary into the bushes. He retrieved it and set it about a yard inside the boundary. "Oh, come on," I shouted. "That's not fair. You have to hit it from where it landed."

"Look at the rules," said Elijah. "This is not golf."

I saw heads turn in our direction, which made me realize we had been shouting. "Okay. You know better than
me," I said in a softer voice.

He won the game, and we sat down on one of the
greener patches of the lawn. "You didn't let me win because you feel sorry for me, did you?" said Elijah.

"You always win. You're even better than... uh... everybody."

"Jason thought it was a sissy game."

"Are you okay?"

"Yeah. I guess."

"Are you sure?"

"Well, I kind of wanted to talk to you about something."

"Sure. No problem."

"You have to promise not to tell anyone else."

That's a tough opening. It puts the listener in a terrible
bind. On the one hand, you're crazy to know what the
secret is, and on the other, you feel like it could be too
much responsibility. If it's something particularly juicy,
how are you ever going to keep it to yourself? "I promise."

"You know in my poem when I said Jason told me if I
told anyone I'd die?"

"Yeah. I suppose he didn't want anyone to know he was
crying because crying is for girls."

"But why was he crying?"

"I guess that's the secret you're going to tell me."

"One night he had a friend, Eric, from the football team
spend the night. They were like best friends. I slept on
the couch in the living room and let Eric have my bed. I
woke up in the middle of the night and Dad was yelling.

He called Eric's parents and had them come and get him. After they left, Dad continued to yell at Jason. When things calmed down, I went back into my room. I asked him if he was okay. He told me to shut up and get out. The way his voice sounded, I could tell he had been crying. 'It's my room too,' I said. I got in my bed and waited. After a little while, he turned over and said, 'We weren't doing anything, just, you know, messing around. He was the one that got in my bed and we were wrestling. We ended up jacking each other off. Lots of guys do it. It's no big deal,' he said."

That was a shocker. Between the two brothers, if anyone suspected one of them was gay, it definitely would have been Elijah. Elijah was quiet and shy, the classical nice guy. So much for stereotypes. "Do you think Jason was gay?"

He hesitated and let out a big sigh. "It wasn't the first time I thought that was possible. He and Eric were always hanging out, and he talked about him all the time. Me and Eric did this. Me and Eric did that. Of course, after that night, Eric was banned from the house. I didn't hear him talk about Eric after that. It happened about a week before we went to that party in Santa Cruz. That's probably why he was so antisocial."

I managed to keep my promise about Elijah's secret for less than two hours. In the car on the way home, I had to tell my dads.

"Is it always bad to tell a secret you've sworn to keep?" I began as we got on the Bay Bridge. Again, with an opening like that, the conversation was only going in one direction.

"What's on your mind, mijo," said Papi.

"Elijah told me something about Jason and made me promise not to tell, but I think it's important."

"Important how?" said Dad.

"Jason was so desperate for his father's approval, which I think adds to and maybe explains the tragedy. You guys should have a good perspective on it."

"Why us?"

"Well, Bart caught Jason messing around with another guy, his best friend."

"That's a lot more common among teenage boys than people like to admit," said Papi.

"But Elijah said he saw other things that made him suspect Jason might be gay."

"I imagine Bart freaked out when he caught Jason with his friend," said Dad.

"Elijah said he was super angry, called the kid's parents and made them come and get him. He told Jason he wasn't allowed to hang out with him anymore."

"That breaks my heart," said Dad. "Jason must have been desperate to get his father's love back."

"He was probably anxious all along, even from a young age, afraid his father wouldn't love him," said Papi. "I went through a period like that with my dad. I was afraid if he found out I was gay, he would throw me out of the house."

"Did you know at Jason's age?" I asked.

"I had a pretty good idea, but I did the usual stuff of denial, like having a girlfriend."

"I was lucky," said Dad. "Nana and Pops let me know early on they supported me no matter what. It still wasn't easy, though. You have to deal with the kids at school."

"What do you think about Devlin?" Things got very quiet in the front seat. I could see the muscles in the back of Dad's neck tense up.

"Devlin is also fortunate to have open-minded parents. And like a lot of young people, he doesn't like to be labeled. So, if you're asking if he's gay, I can't give you an answer. I suppose he's somewhere in that LGBTQIA+ spectrum. How do you feel about that?"

"I love Devlin like a brother. Whatever he does is cool with me." I wanted to add the exception that if he did anything to come between my dads, I was NOT cool with it. But I realized that might sound strange, and it was really something they had to work out.

Seventeen

The summer dragged on with most things closed and Jason's death on everyone's mind. Our proposed trip to England was, of course, not happening. I still spoke to Olivia a lot, but I sometimes wondered how long we could keep it going if we couldn't see each other. In other news, AJ was still having a hard time getting out of bed and ate very little. Dad said he was worried about her. He and Lio would go over and spend time with her and take her out for walks, but it was Elijah who mostly took care of her and kept things going in the house. My dads said Elijah had grown up about ten years in a few weeks and suggested he come over to spend a couple of days to get a break while Lio took over.

Elijah and I were in the back playing Around the World. Since summer activities were limited and my basketball skills were getting rusty, I begged my dads to get one of those portable basketball hoops, and we found a used one online. We had a small, paved area in the back of the house where we set it up.

"Have you seen your dad?" I asked Elijah. He missed his shot badly.

"No. He called once. I didn't know what to say, so I

asked about his injuries. He said he was recuperating and could get up and walk around but didn't leave the house. There was a long pause, and then he started crying. He said he hoped I didn't hate him. I told him I didn't. He kept crying and saying how he had screwed everything up, but he loved me and was going to stop drinking and make some big changes in his life. It made me feel bad, and I wanted to get off the phone, but I stayed on because he's my dad. I didn't tell mom he called, of course."

I felt bad for asking about his dad because it obviously upset him. But it also seemed like he wanted to talk about it. "That must have been hella grim. Let's take a break." I went inside and came back with a couple of sodas. He was sitting on a bench, staring at the ball in his lap.

"I feel bad for my dad, but I have to focus on Mom right now. I've been doing online cooking classes and I think I'm turning out to be a pretty good cook. At least, that's what Mom and Lio say. I've got plenty of time to do that. Lio takes me shopping and I come home and follow the directions carefully. Mom doesn't take more than a few bites of anything, but I try to pay attention to what she likes and come up with new recipes. She drinks a lot of wine. I guess it helps her with the pain."

"You should teach my dads a few tricks. Neither of them cooks very well."

"It's just following the directions. The biggest thing I learned from the online classes is to take your time. Don't rush It."

"I'm doing a lot of online stuff, too, mostly screwing around, but I've found some sites where I can work on my Spanish. My dads had the great idea when I was little that we would spend a few hours every day speaking Spanish, so I would be bilingual. That was a total fail. I guess it sounded good in principle, but hard to put in practice. I've picked up a few things when we go down to visit Papi's family in Los Angeles, but my cousins mostly teach me the bad words, or maybe those are just the ones I remember. They find it really entertaining to hear me use bad words and laugh at me, but they also tell me my pronunciation is pretty good."

"Like what?"

"No mames guey. It's like don't mess with me."

"No mommies way?"

I laughed. "Close enough."

"What's another one?"

"Pinche cabrón! That means real asshole. But you can also say pinche pendejo."

"Pinchy CAB-ron!"

"Okay. You need to work on your pronunciation."

"I want to take Spanish in high school."

"You'd better not use these words in class. I'm taking Spanish, but in the second semester, we're still on me llamo Colton."

"I want to be able to talk to Mom's friend online."

"The guy in Mexico? Is she still chatting with him?"

"Not now. Not since Jason... he's calling her, but she won't answer. One time when Mom was sleeping, I answered her phone."

"No way, dude! My dads would kill me if I did that."

"I know. Mom used to be happy after she talked to him,

so I thought maybe I should tell him what's going on. I introduced myself. He knew a lot about me and asked me questions about school and stuff. His name is Chato. He said he was sorry about Jason."

"So, he knew about that?"

"He said Lio told him. When he was in the States, he and Lio shared an apartment for a few months. He had to go back to Mexico because of immigration issues."

"How come you didn't meet him?"

"He said Mom didn't want Jason and me to know about him because she was going through the divorce."

"Is he like her boyfriend?"

"I don't know. Mom says he's just a friend. All I care about is that she starts feeling better."

"The next time you talk to him, say hola, como estas? Let's get back to our game."

I didn't want to press Elijah too much about his mom's mysterious Mexican friend. It's really none of my business. I took my shot, and it was a swisher. "Three points!" I yelled. "No mames guey!"

"Pinchy CAB-ron!" he said.

The next day, Lio came over to pick up Elijah and drive him back to Oakland. He had texted me that I was going with them and he had a surprise for me. I thought it might be hair-related because he had taken me to get my hair cut before, but I knew salons and barbershops were closed. I was making an effort to take care of it myself, but most of the time, my hair was a bunch of long, unruly curls.

When I was growing up, my dads always kept my hair

short. Wash and go style. But when I was around ten and becoming more aware of my Black identity, I started growing my hair out. Let's face it, part of our Blackness is the coarse and kinky hair that makes us different from other people. My dads allowed me to grow it out but told me I had to learn to take care of it. I soon found out a longer style came with a price: hair care and the time, energy and products that went into it. They bought me a conditioner for type 4 hair and a wide-tooth comb. Mornings I would wake up with serious bed head and would be lazy about combing it out. It was frizzy and didn't look good. At breakfast, Dad and Papi would shake their heads. Dad had more sympathy because he inherited that dark Mediterranean curly hair. He was a classic type three, but his hair was much finer. Papi's hair was thick, but very straight. I kept telling him he could do some serious spiky styles, but he ignored me.

"We have to do something?" said Dad, like it was a major crisis. I was about a year into my longer hair. Lio to the rescue. He took me to a woman who did Black hair in Oakland. I think he was dating her at the time. She taught me how to take care of my hair and educated me about hair types. I was a 4C—thick, bold afro with tight coils on each strand of hair. She fixed me up with products. The last time I went to her I got cornrows. It took a long time, and it was expensive. A few days later, I decided I didn't like it and took it all out.

There were few things that made Papi cross. Wasting money was one of them. "We just spent all this money on a three-day hair style and now it looks worse than ever." He was right. I was now a super frizzy carpet head. I called Lio and told him that Dad and Papi were mad at me about my hair. He came over and took me to Lettie, who cut it short on the sides and squared it on top. She went through the whole care routine again and made me repeat everything.

When Lio, Elijah, and I crossed the Bay Bridge, Lio told me that we were going to Lettie's, but not the salon. It was all hush-hush, like we were breaking the law. We dropped off Elijah and went to Lettie's house.

We all wore masks, but I could still tell she had a big smile for me. "What are we going to do this time?"

I took out my phone and showed her a picture of Devlin. "That's what I want." I had been thinking about it since he came to visit.

"Who's that handsome devil?" she said.

I told her the whole story of meeting Devlin and Olivia in Thailand.

"Looks like they're doing the same styles over there. So, you want to twist it out?"

"Yeah, but I need something that will last and look good for a while so my dads won't get on my case."

"The great thing about this style is that we can do a tight twist at first, and then after a few days or a week, you can untwist it. But it will still look good and curly. Wait 'til your British girlfriend sees it. She'll love it."

"She'll have to see it on video. Who knows when it will be in person?"

She washed my hair and conditioned it. Then she worked in a leave-in conditioner. Next, she showed me a new styling gel she used. "You need to get some of this stuff."

She dried my hair and started running her hair fingers through it, stretching out the strands and combing out the tangles at the same time. Now, to make your hair look good takes a lot of work, but when you have someone else do it, it feels so good (except for the occasional resistant tangle) that you want to drift off into dreamland.

She put more product in my hair, like a ton, and started grabbing strands. She twisted them tight, let them go, and went on to the next. After going through my whole head, she turned the chair around. I loved it. Exactly what I wanted. She showed me how I could unravel the twist and then twist them back if I wanted.

After getting my new do, Lio took me over to the Remember Them: Champions of Humanity Monument in Henry J. Kaiser Park. We had planned to go by there on the day of the BLM march, but that plan got horribly sidetracked. The sculptures commemorate heroes who fought for human rights, a lot of them from the civil rights movement like Martin Luther King, Malcolm X, and Rosa Parks. Lio was proud that he had grown up in Oakland and talked about how the Black Panther Party was centered in Oakland, not in the part of Oakland where he grew up, I'm sure. When I heard Black Panther, the first thing that came to my mind was the movie. "I'm still a little unclear how the movie was related to the Black Panther Party."

"The movie was based on the comic book series," said Lio. "A lot of the ideas in the comics came from the Black

Power movement."

"Can we see where those Oakland parts were filmed? I love that scene where the boys are playing basketball on the playground and that big ol' ship from Wakanda came down from the sky. Those kids freaked. I so wanted to get on that ship."

"Hate to tell ya, my man. Those scenes in the projects weren't filmed in Oakland. I think it was Atlanta."

"Dang. Burst my bubble. Oakland's still cool, though."

Then he took me to the House of Chicken and Waffles in Jack London Square for chicken and waffles. I stuffed myself, and Lio had a big smile on his face, watching me.

"I've got to go shopping for AJ and Elijah, so I need to take you home. How did you like your soul day in Oakland?"

"You're pretty cool for a white guy."

He laughed and grabbed a hunk of his thick, curly brown hair. "I bet I could do my hair like yours."

"It would look good. And, seriously, thanks for every-thing. I loved hanging out with you."

"Me too. We'll do it again soon."

Eighteen

I'm sure I wasn't the first kid born as a result of a cocktail, but the cocktail I'm talking about is quite different from the margaritas my dads often have when we go out to eat or the mimosas they serve to their friends when they come over for Sunday brunch. It had become our family joke that I was a cocktail baby since that day they explained how I came into the world. Most kids go happily along, not thinking much about where they came from. Little by little they get information about the birds and the bees (I never understood where that expression came from) through siblings or cousins or sex education classes or their parents sitting them down for "the talk" like mine did or nowadays the Internet if you didn't have parents who were tech aware enough to block access to certain sites. Very often it's a combination of those information sources, after which you end up with a confusing mix of truth, fiction, and fantasy.

In my case, it was a little different. That time we were visiting Papi's family, and I wandered off (or my cousins deliberately took me to another house and left me), I still remember what someone said when Dad came to the doorway of the house where I was. It was burned into my brain. Someone pointed at him and said, "That's his daddy." And another person said, "No. That can't be his daddy. He's white."

"He is my daddy," I said, running to him, crying because I was so happy to be reunited, but also because of what that kid said, putting this weird kind of doubt in my little head. I didn't even understand what the doubt was. It was just a feeling. All my cousins, on the other hand, could look at their parents and know they were their moms and dads because they looked like them. The parents would constantly say things like, "she is tan linda como su mamá" or "he acts exactamente como su papá."

When my dads felt I was ready for the sex talk, it was pretty hard for it not to drift into the conversation of where I came from and the revelation of the "cock-tail." Dad explained how a man's penis had to go into an opening in a woman's body and shoot in sperm to fertilize an egg inside her body. I had already gotten some of that from other sources, and after that incident with Jason calling me the n-word, I knew that the woman who carried me for nine months was named Joy and she was Black. So, my next question was logical.

"Did one of you do that to Joy?"

"Not exactly," said Papi. "Sex isn't the only way for a woman to get pregnant."

I must have looked confused, and Dad took over. "I'm sure you've had the sensation of your penis getting hard, an erection. When you get older, I doubt it's happened yet, that can lead to a fluid coming out called semen. Sometimes it can happen spontaneously when you're sleeping, and we call that a wet dream."

Boy, talk about beating around the bush. "Uh, Dad. My question?"

"Yeah, well, my point is you don't have to have sex to ejaculate semen. You can do it yourself."

"Jacking off?"

"Oh, so, you know about that."

"Yes, Dad."

"Okay. Papi and I did that and mixed it together into what we jokingly called a cocktail. Joy inserted it into her vagina, and my little buddies and Papi's little buddies raced to see which one would get to the egg first so the pregnancy would begin."

"Little buddies? Really, Dad."

He giggled. "I know. Anyway, we decided that we didn't want to know whose little buddies got there first because it didn't matter which of us was your actual biological father. We were both your dads and would love and take care of you just the same."

"So, you still don't know?"

"Nope," said Papi.

"How did you do it because you said she was living in Los Angeles, right? Could you send your little buddies through the mail?"

"No way," said Papi. "You have to get the stuff inside her warm body right away. It's tricky because when you do it the way we did, it often doesn't work the first time. Or the second or the third. We kept having to fly down to LA when Joy was ovulating, you know, producing eggs. We stayed with my parents and would go over to Joy's house for a few hours. My parents would look at us funny and kept saying it was nice to have so many visits, but after the fourth or fifth time, they got a little suspicious. We didn't want to tell them what we were doing until it actually worked."

"There's also a process a little more reliable called in vitro insemination where they combined the egg and sperm in a lab outside the mother and then insert the embryo in the woman's body a few days later," said Dad. "But it's very expensive. We didn't have that kind of money."

"Oh, so I was not just a cocktail baby, I was a bargain baby." At first, I thought I may have crossed a line, but they both laughed.

"And what a bargain you were!" said Dad. "You know my people like a good bargain." I was a little shocked he said that, but I guess, being Jewish, he could say stuff like that.

It wasn't particularly comfortable having this sex talk with my dads, but I had to appreciate they were willing to talk about it. When I compared notes with kids at school, a lot of them said their parents never mentioned the word sex, let alone gave them the talk. Another thing was happening in the back of my head while my parents were going on about penises and wet dreams and how they made the cocktail. If I had turned out gay, I wondered what the sex talk would have been like. I'm sure there would have been a version of the condom (also known as a little buddy blocker) demo (my dads used a cucumber because we were out of bananas), but with a special emphasis on venereal diseases, and, of course, HIV. Clearly, everybody has to worry about sexually transmitted diseases, but my dads told me they started being sexually active at a time a lot of people were still dying of AIDS, and it really left a strong impression on them.

Then they might have gone into the mechanics of gay sex. Something like: a man's erect penis goes into an opening… stop! I didn't want to go there. Not about my dads. So, my brain, in its lame attempt to steer me in a different direction, headed down a path that was almost as bad. That day when Fer made the comment about Josh breaking up with me wasn't completely off the wall and my angry response wasn't just a reaction to Fer being out of line and might have been considered an over-reaction. Dad loved to use the phrase, "Me thinks thou doth protest too much," when my protesting was a little over the top, especially when he knew I knew I was in the wrong. He says it comes from Shakespeare. Typical Dad.

After Josh's mom and dad broke up, his dad and new girlfriend liked to go fishing and camping, but Josh hated to go with them alone. A couple of times his dad let him invite Fer and me. It was really fun. The three of us slept in a small tent and talked about stupid things and made fart jokes since we usually had beans for dinner. Of course, we'd talk about sex and Josh told us his girlfriend gave him a blow job, going into a lot of detail. He liked to build himself up telling us stuff like that, but at the same time loved to razz Fer about not getting any from his girlfriend, Carmen.

One night, Fer got pissed and rolled over. "I'm done."

Josh and I kept talking and laughing. Fer told us to shut up and go to sleep. We eventually settled down, and it sounded like Josh had drifted off to sleep. But not me. On top of having to smell Josh's stinky socks, I had the hornies so bad I thought I might have to choke the chicken right there in the sleeping bag. Not a good option. Josh was inches away. As quietly as I could, I unzipped my sleeping bag, put on my shoes, unzipped the tent flap, and crawled out onto the ground. I shivered with cold, but I was on an important mission. Since that first time I made myself cum about six months before, it had become a little out of control. Thank God, from an early age, my dads had me doing my own laundry. I thought they didn't notice I was washing my sheets a lot, but, of course, they did and had to snicker about it to boot.

I started walking toward the lake and I didn't even need my cell phone light because there was a full moon. I got near the water and saw the moon reflecting on the surface and smelled the pine trees and heard the little waves lapping at the shore. Everything was so beautiful I forgot what I was there for. NOT. I couldn't wait to get my hand in my pants and get this over with and go back to my warm sleeping bag because all I had on was a T-shirt, and I was freezing my ass off. It took me two seconds to get hard. Let the stroking games begin.

Damn! Was that a cracking branch I just heard? I paused. Someone was definitely walking up behind me. I wilted. Damn. Damn. Damn.

Josh whispered, "What are you doing?"

"Peeing."

He came up next to me and looked at my crotch. "You don't look like you're peeing."

"I finished."

He bent down and looked at the ground. "I guess it was a dry pee." He started laughing. "You were jacking off."

"No, I wasn't"

"Dude. It's cool. Why are you embarrassed?"

"I don't know."

He put his hand on his dick. "You wanna suck my cock?"

I was pissed. Did he think that since I grew up with gay dads I got home training in how to suck cock? "No. You wanna suck my cock?"

"No. Guess we'll just have to do a side by side."

"No way," I said, even though I was starting to get hard again. "I'm going back."

He grabbed my arm. "No. Wait."

He had his thing out and was stroking it slowly with his other hand. "Don't make me do it alone. It's cool. Lots of guys do it."

My hard-on was raging, but I was afraid if he saw it, he would think I was hard for him. I wrenched my arm from his grip and took a step away from him but didn't leave. I stared at the lake and used all my power not to watch what he was doing.

It took about a minute for him to grunt and shoot. He stood there a minute, shaking it before putting it away. "Awesome!" he said. "Now you."

"I can't."

"Take it out damnit!"

Josh was the kind of guy that liked a lot of contact with

his buddies, but you never thought it was in a gay way. He put his arm around Fer's and my shoulders all the time and pulled us close, said things in our ears. Josh was good-looking and popular, and he had a way of pulling people in and making them feel special. On the court, he would pat us on the butt. In the showers, he would be the one to drop the soap, and say, "Hey, Cole, could you get me that soap?" He was always horsing around.

He got behind me and put his hands on my shoulders. He moved close, so close I could feel the heat radiating off his body as he whispered in my ear. "Come on. You can do it." His breath tickled my ear. It sent chills up and down my spine, and yes, it was hot.

It didn't take me long to spill all over the ground.

"Good boy," he said. "I mean, good man." He laughed again. He seemed totally relaxed, and I felt the opposite. This creepy shame was rising in my stomach, even though we hadn't done anything that would be considered sexual, like contact sex. I became afraid he would tell someone what we had done and say it was me who initiated it. But he wasn't that kind of guy. He wasn't a bully or one of those guys always stirring up trouble. He was just funny and playful, and always a good friend. Until he wasn't. Yes, it hurt when he ratted me out and then dumped me.

We walked back to the tent in silence. We crawled in, and Fer woke up. "Where were you guys?"

"Had to pee," said Josh.

Josh and I never talked about it, but I once had a dream where he was blowing in my ear and I woke up with a big hardon. The jackoff incident was the last time we went camping together. A few months later, the Target thing happened.

One evening late in the summer of Jason's death and the pandemic and the lockdown and general boredom, Dad called me to the dinner table and set a large bowl of spaghetti and meatballs he had thrown together with sauce from a jar and packaged meatballs from the frozen section. In pandemic mode, he and Papi took turns cooking while it was my job to clean up. We hadn't been to a restaurant in months, though we did takeout on Sundays.

I was in a bad mood. I took one look at the food and said, "Too bad Devlin isn't here to cook."

"Anytime you want to start cooking, be my guest," said Dad.

Papi waved his hands in a cutting motion to cancel Dad's suggestion. "Be careful what you ask for."

I plopped down in my chair. "I can cook. Maybe I should do some online cooking classes like Elijah is doing."

Throughout the meal, Papi was very quiet. He filled his plate, but barely touched it.

"I know it's not very good," said Dad. "Should I make something else? There might be a frozen pizza in there?"

Papi's face looked like he was in pain. "No. I'm just not hungry." He scooted his chair back and put his hand to his chest. "I don't feel very well. I'm going to lie down."

"What is it, Papi?" I said.

He rose to his feet, but he looked confused like he was dizzy. "I... I'm having trouble breathing."

"Should I call the doctor?" Dad said.

"No, I'll be fine. I just need to lie down."

After he left the room, Dad and I looked at each other with fear plastered on our faces. Thanks to the pandemic, anytime someone got a little sniffle or a headache or the tiniest tummy ache, the word covid immediately started flashing in your brain like a neon sign. But when someone grabs his chest and says he's having trouble breathing, absolute panic takes over. There were too many stories in the news about people going into the hospital and never coming out, stories about people not being able to say goodbye to loved ones.

"I'll go check on him," said Dad.

I sat at the table and stared at the spaghetti. The strange thing was that I was hungry, but I took a bite, and ended up spitting it out, and not because it tasted bad. I had this sinking feeling in my stomach, which hit the floor when Dad came back in and said he was calling 911. And then I began having shortness of breath and a heart beating in a weird way, but I knew it was because I was scared, not the kind of sickness like I was coming down with something. I started toward the hallway.

"Where are you going?" said Dad.

"I'm going to check on Papi."

Dad came over to me and pulled me into a hug. "I know you want to see Papi, but we should probably stay out of the room in case..." He couldn't finish. He took a deep, shaky breath. "Screw it. Let's go."

We went into the bedroom and sat by the bed with Papi until the medics came. He continued having trouble breathing and every few minutes he would rise up and cough. He was scared. We were scared. I tried not to cry. It was the worst day of my life.

Medics came in all geared up like they were the cleanup crew for a nuclear disaster. We put on masks, but it was probably too late for that. They gave Papi oxygen and took him away on a stretcher. Dad held his hand until they had to separate, like that Michelangelo painting of Adam and God in the Sistine Chapel. It broke my heart.

From AJ's horrible experience at the emergency room, we knew they wouldn't let us in, so we didn't follow to the hospital. They had already told us that we couldn't ride with him in the back of the ambulance. We watched them turn on the flashing light and pull away from the curb, taking the person away from us we both loved the most. We went back inside and collapsed on the couch, sobbing.

Dad called all his siblings. Lio offered to come over, but Dad said there was nothing he could do. He didn't call Papi's family because he thought we should wait and see for sure. I heard Dad say to M, "I just don't understand. We've been so careful." And then it hit me. Dad and Papi barely left the house. I was out and about much more than they were. Fer came over occasionally and we played basketball in the back. I was the one who went to the corner store if we needed bread or milk or something. If covid had come into the house, I was probably the one who brought it in. On top of my sadness, I now felt a terrible guilt. Needless to say, neither of us slept that night. Dad kept calling the hospital, but he couldn't get through. Early in the morning, after the sun came up, I fell asleep from exhaustion. I don't know how long I was asleep, but I woke up to Dad yelling at someone over the phone. I jumped out of bed.

"What's happening, Dad?"

He held up his hand to me, gave the sign for one minute, and then continued shouting at the person on the phone. "I need someone to call me immediately and tell me what's going on." He got off the phone and looked at me with red eyes. "Sorry, honey. Nobody will tell me anything."

"What about Arnie? Can't he find out something?" Arnie was a doctor at Kaiser, where they had taken Papi.

"M called him this morning, and he's supposed to get back to me. Do you want some breakfast?"

I had only had a couple of hours of sleep. I was knackered, as Devlin would say. "I'm going back to bed. Wake me up as soon as you hear anything."

At some time in the afternoon, Dad came into my room. I woke up, and he was sobbing. Oh, God, no! I thought.

And then, through his tears, a smile came across his face. "It's okay. He's okay. It's not covid." I sat up and we hugged, bawling our eyes out. "Arnie called me. They found a pulmonary embolism. They're not sure what caused it."

"That sounds like it could be worse."

"It's like a blood clot in his lungs. He needs to rest, but they'll probably send him home tomorrow. Being in the hospital is about the worst place you can be right now."

"I thought I had brought covid into the house. I freaked. If anything happened, it would have been my fault."

"I'm sorry you were suffering with that guilt. I know you've been careful and good about wearing a mask. As my mom used to say, viruses don't have names on them."

"It really makes you wonder, though."

"We're all doing the best we can. But, I suppose, with this little scare, we have to be even more careful."

"I can't wait to have him home."

"Me too. We should have something to eat. We haven't eaten in like twenty-four hours."

When Papi came home from the hospital the next day, we bombarded him with so many smiles and hugs he said, "Enough already. You make me feel like Lazarus arisen from the dead."

"Who's Lazarus?" I asked.

Dad started to jump in to explain as usual and then caught himself. "Honey, you want to give our son a little Bible lesson?" Papi had grown up in a Christian house where Bible lessons came with the territory. Dad knew about Lazarus because, well, he knew about everything.

Papi looked tired and his breathing was still a little off, but he was anxious for the opportunity to show what he knew for a change. "Lazarus was a friend of Jesus, and when Jesus heard the news that Lazarus had died, he made the journey to Bethany. Jesus went to the grave where all his relatives were still mourning and told the people to roll away the stone in front of his tomb. Lazarus's sister objected because she was afraid of the smell. Good thing I didn't get to the smelly stage."

"Oh, Papi. Come on."

"So, they did what he told them because, you know, he was Jesus. They removed the stone, and lo and behold, Lazarus walks out of the tomb as alive as you and me. It was said to be the last miracle Jesus performed before he was crucified. We'll save the crucifixion story for another day."

We didn't leave the house for the next three days. We played games, watched movies, laughed, told stories, and spent every minute Papi was awake with him. We ate frozen pizza and ordered food to be delivered. It's kind of sad that it takes a scare like that to make you realize what you have. Before Papi got sick, we had fallen into the trap of boredom and frustration about what was happening in the world. None of us was in a particularly good space and, at times, were a little crabby with each other. Papi's illness was the classic wake up call.

In the days that Papi was in the hospital and the following days when he came home, I was so caught up in the drama, I didn't communicate with Olivia. I finally looked at her messages, and the last one said, 'Are you breaking up with me?' That was kind of weird because we had never said officially that we were boyfriend and girlfriend, though it was definitely implied.

I called her and told her what had happened. She apologized for the dramatic text and sent Papi best wishes for his recovery. Soon after that, Joanna called and then Devlin called. Everyone expressed how happy they were that it wasn't something more serious and it made me realize how in the short time our two families were together in Thailand, we had grown closer than a lot of people were with their blood relatives.

Back to the cocktail. A few days after Papi came home from the hospital, his doctor called with the results of all the tests they had run on him. What caused the blood clots was called Factor V Leiden, a mutation in the clotting factors in the blood. More commonly, the clots in this condition happen in the legs and what happened to Papi was rare. The big news was that it was hereditary. There was no cure, but they could lower the risks of future complications by keeping an eye on it and having him take blood thinners. She asked if Papi knew of anyone else in his family who had the condition. Papi wasn't aware of it. The doctor also knew Papi had a son, but I don't think she knew the circumstances. She said it would be a good idea if I got tested for the condition, but unfortunately, our medical plan wouldn't pay for it. It wasn't something to be terribly concerned about, she said, but it was always good to know if I had this mutation (scary word like monsters and stuff). Papi had neglected to mention in the conversation with his doctor that he wasn't certain he was the biological father.

After our three-day lovefest, we had a serious issue to consider. We sat down after dinner to talk about it. Apparently, they had discussed Joy's family history at length before they made the final decision to have her as the surrogate mom. They admitted they hadn't been so diligent about themselves. There was one fairly inexpensive way to determine if Factor V Leiden was even something we had to worry about. We could do one of those mail-in DNA tests that would tell us if I had Jewish Italian/Hungarian/ Romanian ancestry or Spanish/Mexican/Indigenous ancestry. Of course, we knew from Joy's side we would get mainly African. For a hundred bucks, we would have peace of mind in one area, but it would open up a whole new can of worms. I would no longer be a cocktail baby, but definitively either Dad's or Papi's biological son. I know, heavy. But the more I thought about it, there was no way the results would change how I felt about my dads. They were legally and emotionally and in every way possible my parents. Both of them. Forever.

For them, I had a feeling it wasn't so simple. They had grown so attached over the years to the cocktail baby idea that letting it go might be delicate. They had made a little joke about the little buddies racing to the egg, but if they knew one of them 'won' would it make a difference? I didn't think so, but I had seen stranger things happen. I would never have imagined losing Josh's friendship over the Target incident or losing a cousin because his dad had become such a troglodyte. I would never have imagined that Aunt M would become Uncle M or AJ would have a boyfriend in Mexico or a blind guy could become a DJ or Jason might have been gay or Olivia would get mad at me because I said I liked fish and chips, which we called French fries instead of chips or Papi would lose it when Devlin hugged Dad, making me wonder if maybe Dad liked Devlin a little too much. Basically, every day brought something new and complicated into our lives and a lot of it we'll probably never understand.

To be perfectly honest, I was curious about a test that would tell me something about my ancestry. But I didn't want to say that because I didn't want to influence the decision one way or the other. My dads went back and forth, talking about the advantages and disadvantages, but mostly assuring each other that it didn't matter who the biological father was.

"The test could tell us other medical information beyond whether he might have the Factor V Leiden mutation," said Dad.

"So, you think he should do the test," said Papi.

"Only if you agree." And then he thought for a minute. "Maybe we should all do the test."

"That's an interesting idea," said Papi. "What do you think, Cole?"

"Okay. I'm curious, but not about the little buddies. We could all find out more about where we came from and even learn what part of Africa Joy's ancestors were from. Maybe she's a distant relative of Cleopatra. I read something that said the queen of Egypt might have been Black."

"I don't think the results are that specific," said Dad. "It just tells you what percentage of your DNA comes from different geographic regions and the main population groups in those areas."

"This girl at school did it and made a report. Her parents are Salvadorean, but she was surprised to find she had a high percentage of Ashkenazi Jewish DNA."

"People are often surprised because the information handed down in families doesn't always jive with the DNA results, not that the different ancestry companies are a hundred percent correct."

Papi sighed. "We're getting a little off the topic. Are we going to do it or not?"

"You guys have to swear," I said, "that you won't care whose buddies got there first."

"I swear," said Papi.

"I swear," said Dad.

We got the kits and spent an afternoon spitting saliva into a tube. I spit and spit and spit, only to hold up the tube and see that it was a quarter filled. Papi and Dad did the same. We all looked at each other like for a dollar, we'd give the whole thing up. The only thing that kept us going was that we had already spent three hundred dollars on the kits, but at least it covered the cost of the test. We bucked up our courage and spit some more. The other downside of the test was that we would have to wait four to six weeks for the results. I hadn't really thought about that. I had imagined being able to call up Olivia the following week and tell her I was half Chinese. The wait began. Another depressing note was that we would be back in school by the time we got the results. And when I say back in school, I mean online classes. The district said they would not consider in-class instruction until at least 2021. In the spring, I had been, at first, excited about not having to get up so early and do the long walk to school. But the stay-at-home thing got boring pretty quickly. It also meant no basketball, and I missed the guys on the team, even the coach who was a wanker sometimes, and I do mean in the asshole sense.

Not in the other sense. No scandal here.

Nineteen

It was the middle of September. Papi was back to normal and walking about five miles a day. I was spending way too much time on the computer and other devices. Between online classes, chatting with Olivia, playing video games, following what was going on with the election, and checking on the latest covid statistics, it was getting ridiculous. My dads said I was turning into a zombie, not to mention that my muscles were probably going to shrivel up until I couldn't walk. Okay, the last part got to me. I was already feeling guilty for not keeping up with the exercises Devlin taught me. What could I cut out? School was obligatory, and no way was I going to stop chatting with Olivia. I figured I could cut down on the video games, but the politics and the covid statistics research were the most likely candidates for the trash bin.

There was one thing I wanted to add to my screen time, though I thought I could keep it to a minimum. I was serious about improving our dinner options by learning how to make a few dishes. I called and asked Elijah for his easiest, no-fail recipe.

"You should try arroz con pollo. That means chicken

with rice," said Elijah.

"Uh, hello? I taught you your first words in Spanish. I know what arroz con pollo means."

He chuckled. "Oh, that's right. Anyway, you only taught me dirty words."

"Can you walk me through it? I'm sick of frozen pizza and takeout Chinese."

"Get a chicken cut into pieces. Put some oil in a pan and brown the chicken."

"What do you mean, brown?"

"Oh, man. I gotta tell you everything? You cook the chicken in the oil, medium-high heat until it turns brown. It's okay if it's not cooked all the way through. Take it out and put in on a plate. Then sauté onions and red bell pepper in the same oil. When they're cooked, put a couple of cups of rice in the pan. That should be enough to have leftovers for a few days."

"You mean cooked rice."

"No dry."

"No way."

"Trust and believe. Sauté it with the veggies. It will turn kind of brown, too. Then you add a whole carton of chicken broth, salt, pepper, garlic, and any other herbs you want. Then put the chicken pieces back in the pan and stir them in with everything. Turn the heat to low and cover the pan until all the liquid is absorbed by the rice."

"I don't know. That sounds complicated."

"Nah. You can do it. Let me know how it comes out. Call me if you get stuck in the middle."

We sounded like a pair of housewives discussing

recipes on the phone. Aren't parents supposed to provide delicious and nutritious meals for their kids? What was happening here?

After watching several YouTube cooking videos, I felt brave enough to tell my dads I was going to make dinner. They gave each other worried looks. "I got this," I said. "I have instructions from Chef Elijah."

I was so proud of myself when I put the pan on the table and lifted the lid. Steam and a wonderful aroma of arroz con pollo lifted into the air.

"Smells good," said Papi. "Your abuela used to make arroz con pollo all the time. I promise I won't compare, though."

I was on pins and needles when they took their first bites. I was pleased there was no retching or expressions of agony on their faces. Dad nodded his head and smiled. "This is pretty good. Great job, my son. You're hired."

"Your abuela would be so proud of you. It's different from hers, but it's delicioso."

I let out a big sigh of relief. "I panicked in the middle of it and had to call Elijah. He talked me down."

"What are cousins for if not to talk you through a recipe?" said Dad.

"We're teenagers. We're supposed to be having fun and getting into trouble."

"I guess we failed the cooking part of getting married and having a kid," said Papi. "It's a miracle you grew as tall and strong as you are."

I flexed my biceps. "Hah! This is pathetic. I need to get back to my workout."

"Hmm. Good in the kitchen and obsessed with muscles. Are you sure you're not gay?"

"That's not funny, Dad."

"Augie, that was a ridiculous thing to say!" said Papi.

"Sorry," said Dad.

"I thought we were beyond stereotypes," I said, all huffy.

"Guys, chill. It was a joke."

I actually thought it was funny and felt a little bad that I was making him squirm just a bit. We finished eating, and I automatically started clearing plates since that was my job.

"Don't worry about it," said Dad. "You cooked, so we'll clean up tonight."

"I guess you guys will be cleaning up for the next couple of nights," I said. "We have lots of leftovers." I put the dishes I had gathered into the sink and stood by the table.

"Don't push it, buddy," said Papi.

"I'm so glad you didn't say little buddy."

They laughed, and it reminded me how much I enjoyed making my dads laugh. But there was a little nervous tick in their laughter. In fact, there had been something off throughout the meal, including Dad's gay comment. They continued sitting at the table with awkward smiles on their faces and without making a move to clean up. "Have a seat," said Dad. His face changed from smiley emoji to serious emoji.

"What?" Would it be good news or bad news?

"Speaking of little buddies," said Dad. "We... uh... got the results of our tests today. The good news is that we don't have to worry about you having the Factor V Leiden mutation."

"Oh," I said, looking at Papi with an I'm-sorry expression. But he still had that strange smile on his face. Maybe he really didn't care. Phew! I was glad the waiting was over, and we could just go back to normal life. Ha ha. Life hadn't been normal for a while. "Is there something else because you guys are being weird?"

"You also don't have any Jewish DNA in your profile," said Dad.

I was confused. "So, you're not really Jewish? That was just one of those family myths that gets handed down?"

"No, I'm pretty sure I'm Jewish."

Papi groaned. "Just tell him."

"Neither of us is your biological father."

"What?" I screamed. "Is this some kind of joke?"

"You don't share any of your DNA with us. At first, I thought it had to be wrong. I did some research and found that though the tests aren't one hundred percent accurate, it would be impossible that they would be one hundred percent wrong. While you were out playing basketball this afternoon, we had a talk with Joy."

"More like a screaming session," said Papi. "I asked your dad to take a little break and let me talk to her alone. How to put this discreetly. Joy was not supposed to have sexual relations with other guys while we were going through the process, but it was taking a long time and she... I guess..."

Dad jumped in. "Long story short, she fucked another guy and got pregnant." He was angry. He never used the

F-word in front of me.

I sat at our wooden table with my dads across the table in our kitchen in the house I had grown up in, but I had been transported to another planet or a parallel universe, everything familiar and yet nothing the same. I felt like I was in one of the Twilight Zone rerun episodes my dads liked to watch, and sometimes I watched with them. My head was spinning, and I felt a little sick. Most of my life, I had gone without any contact with the woman who carried me for nine months. But once I understood how I came into the world, at least I knew I had a blood connection with one of my dads. I know I said I didn't care about all that. I swore I wouldn't care which of them was my biological father. But to find out it was neither of them hit me hard.

"I know this must come as quite a shock," said Dad.

"Understatement," I mumbled.

"It was a shock to us, too, obviously. But, remember, we all agreed that whatever the results, it wouldn't matter."

"Who was the guy?" I asked in an exhausted voice. Was I going to have to go on a new quest for my real father? I didn't think I had it in me. "No. I don't want to know. I don't care. Can I be excused?"

"We'll talk more later," said Papi. "I think that's enough for now."

I went to my room and lay on my bed. I didn't even take off my sneakers, which my dads were always yelling at me about. Adults are such wankers. How did they screw this up? I thought of all the examples of how parents had screwed up their kids' lives in the past year. The more

I thought about it, the angrier I got. Just to spite them, I wasn't going to call them Dad and Papi anymore but Augie and Ruben. See how they'd like that.

The last time I had talked to Olivia, she was furious with her dad because she had put on makeup to go to this party, and he had said she looked slutty. It was settled. I would hop on a plane to London, get Olivia, and we would run off together to... I didn't know where, but we would find a place. Of course, I couldn't call her and tell her about our escape plan because it was like five in the morning there. I would call her later.

At some point, Papi came in after I had fallen asleep. He took off my sneakers and covered me with a blanket. I woke up but kept my eyes closed. He didn't make me get up and take off my clothes or brush my teeth. He kissed me on the top of my head.

In the morning, I got up with a new attitude. I felt foolish and guilty about all the horrible thoughts I'd had about my dads. It wasn't their fault. I knew they had given me more love than any kid could expect from their parents. They weren't like Josh's parents or AJ and Bart. They gave me a beautiful life and didn't deserve my moods and bad behavior.

I went into the kitchen and they had prepared my favorite breakfast: waffles with real maple syrup and bacon. Dad wore this silly apron with butterflies on it, and Papi had flour on his right cheek. "I'm sorry," I said and started to choke up.

"You have nothing to be sorry about. We're sorry."

"Last night I was going to run away to London."

"We would miss you," said Dad.

I smiled. Dad's eyes were red like he hadn't slept and Papi had a scraggily beard and his hair was sticking out every which way. They looked so ridiculous and sad and wonderful. I kind of lost it.

"Come here," said Papi. We had a three-way hug where they let me cry. It was warm and soft and they smelled like my dads and I felt like the luckiest guy in the world.

We sat down to breakfast. "Just so you know," I said. "I'm not going to go looking for my biological father."

"Uh... you can't," said Dad.

"What Augie means is he died in Iraq not long after you were born. This morning Joy sent us an email with a sincere apology. She asked what the DNA results were, and it confirmed what she had suspected but never wanted to say because she hoped it wasn't true. She had met a Puerto Rican guy on leave, and they had an affair around the time she was supposed to be getting pregnant with our baby. She claimed to have miscalculated her cycles."

"She sent a picture, but we can just delete it if you'd rather not see it," said Dad.

"Let me think about it. What did my results show?"

"From the father's side you got about thirty percent West African, a significant percentage of Spanish European and a small percentage of Broadly Northwestern European."

Curiosity got the better of me. "Okay. Show me the picture."

Papi pulled up the picture on his phone. "Joy said he was tall. About six feet."

"And very handsome, as you can see," said Dad.

I stared at the picture. He was in uniform. I looked like him. He had a buzz cut, so I couldn't see what his hair was like, but the eyes and nose were definitely mine. I had always wondered about my height because Joy, Dad, and Papi were all average height. Whenever we had talked about how tall I was (and I wasn't finished growing yet), Dad would always say genetics was quirky. Now, at least one mystery was solved.

"I bet Nana and Pops wouldn't have liked that he was a soldier and served in Iraq."

"Who knows?" said Dad. "Maybe they all met up in heaven and found out they liked each other."

"I thought you didn't believe in heaven."

He shrugged. "Sometimes it's fun to think about it in that way. I like to think of my mom and dad being together in a nice place."

Twenty

In the second week of my new status of being basically an orphan adopted by two gay dads (and I was completely okay with it), I made my second successful meal: lasagna. Elijah gave me the recipe, and it was a lot of fun to make. You get all the ingredients ready—the cooked pasta, the meat sauce, the ricotta, the mozzarella cheese—and then you start building, layer upon layer, like you're building a tower with Legos or something. I got it in the oven and kept checking on it, looking for that crusty top and the bubbling around the sides that Elijah had told me about. When I took it out, I was pleased. At least it looked like lasagna.

We sat down to eat, and I was nervous again about how my dads would like it. Forks up. One, two, three, go. They took bites at the same time. Nodding heads. Chewing. Satisfied swallow. Smiles. Excellent finish.

"This is scrumptious," said Dad.

"It's not too gay for you?"

"It's totally gay," said Dad. "It's Troye Sivan gay, especially with that green stuff mixed in with the ricotta."

"You know who he is now?"

"I have to keep up with my son and my husband. What

is the green stuff?"

"It's spinach."

"And there's a really interesting flavor," said Papi.

"It's probably the nutmeg."

Dad and Papi gave each other a what-monster-have-we-created look.

"You really like it?"

"It's hella good," said Papi, making fun of my frequent use of the adverb.

"You guys don't have to say that. I've abandoned my plan to run off to London."

"Darn," said Dad. "Papi and I thought we were going to get a little peace and quiet."

"You can put me on a plane to England anytime. I won't complain."

"Speaking of, I got an email from Joanna today. They're exhausted with what's happening in England. Olivia's classes are online. Devlin's internship got cancelled. Nigel says his online teaching is tiresome, and Joanna's practice is exclusively online. They had thought about going back to Thailand, but the quarantine restrictions are Draconian. They've decided to go to The Bahamas. That's where Joanna's parents are from. She said we should join them."

"I know," I said. "Olivia told me.

"Why didn't you say anything?"

"I didn't want to hear the no answer."

"I guess I'm out of the loop," said Papi. "Why am I always the last to know?"

Dad and I looked at each other. Did he really want us to answer that? "You were copied on the email," said Dad.

"I haven't looked at my messages in days."

"Joanna said The Bahamas has restrictions, too, but they're more manageable. Test within five days of travel and apply for a travel health visa. After you get there, you have to fill out a daily online questionnaire, and get tested again after five days. But no quarantine. I looked at some flights just for fun."

"No way!" said Papi. "Forget about it, Augie."

"See?" I said.

"We need a break," said Dad. "After all we've been through lately."

"That's ridiculous, even if we could afford it. It's not realistic."

"We got those stimulus checks and haven't spent the money yet."

"I'm sure the government's intention for that money was not to run off to the Caribbean."

"They can't really keep track of how you spend it."

"Anyway, I suppose movement around the islands is limited," said Papi. "We'd be stuck in a hotel room."

"I looked it up. There are the usual precautions of mask wearing, but most of the islands have indoor dining and you are free to roam. The Brits are renting a bungalow on the beach. We could rent one next door. Joanna has a cousin who works in a resort on Andros and can arrange everything. I saw pictures, and it looks fabulous."

"You did all this research without even telling me?"

I was trying hard not to get my hopes up, but Dad was serious. One thing I can say about Dad is that when he puts his mind to something, he usually gets it. "Come on,

Papi," I said. "Think about it."

"You know you wouldn't be able to start with the kissy face on Olivia right away. Or are you going to kiss through a mask?"

"I know, Papi. Don't be gross."

"It may not be as preposterous as it sounds. After the fifth-day Covid test, everyone can relax," said Dad.

"Is Devlin going?" asked Papi with a smirk. "Maybe he'll bring a girlfriend this time." Oh, yeah. In my excitement, I had forgotten the Devlin question. I certainly didn't want to witness any more scenes of Papi's jealousy.

"Of course, he'll be there. Joanna says he's quite excited about it."

"Next, you're going to tell me the island is so cheap we can actually save money by being there."

"There are some good deals on flights and hotels. A lot of places have a reasonable meal plan. They're desperate for tourists."

"Oh my God, this is going to be so much fun!" I said.

"No. This is not happening," said Papi. "I won't be bullied into this."

"The dates they're going overlap with the election. We could mail in our ballots and get the hell out of Dodge. Do you really want to be here for the craziness?"

Papi's face fell into a false agony, a last-ditch effort. "It's hurricane season for God's sake!"

After our conversation, I ran to the phone to call Olivia. "I think we're going to do it."

"Do what?" she said.

"Go to the Bahamas with you."

"Oh, that's been canceled."

"What? No." My voice cracked like a chipmunk trying to sing.

"I'm just messing with you. We already have the tickets."

"That's mean."

She giggled. "I wish I could have seen your face."

"You're cruel. I don't want to go now."

"You are full of it. I've got some great new music for us to listen to."

"Well, I guess the music would be worth it."

"Yay! I can't believe we're going to see each other after so long."

A few weeks later we did see each other's faces again after a covid test, one long, and two short flights, wearing masks for twelve straight hours (or as my dads would say twelve gaily forward hours), and some crappy fast food. We survived a red-eye from San Francisco to Miami, and then the hops to Nassau and then Andros. At the Andros Town airport, a man in a flowery shirt held up a sign with our names, but he had spelled Burd, B-I-R-D and Paniagua with a Y. He led us to a limousine that had seen much better days, but we made it to the resort without a breakdown or flat tire (or flat tyre as our British friends would put it) over some rough roads.

We checked in at the office, and a woman with long cornrow braids took us to our bungalow, one of three bungalows grouped together. Ours was burnt orange, the Saxton's next door was pineapple yellow, and the third was blueberry making a fruit salad against a pale blue sky. The bungalows were right on a wide beach with sugary white sand where a hot breeze, seasoned with that salty, seaweedy smell blew over us. As the woman unlocked the French doors with a view of the ocean, we saw Olivia, Joanna, and Nigel stretched out on lounge chairs in front of their bungalow and Devlin in the water, playing in the waves.

Joanna waved. "Take a moment to get settled," she said, "and come round. We've got champagne on ice."

"You all look lovely," said Dad. "We'll be over in a minute."

I waved at Olivia, but I was embarrassed to do what my thumping heart was telling me, which was to rush over and take her in my arms. After we had all tested negative before we left, Dad reminded me we couldn't be too relaxed until after our fifth-day test on the island because we were going to be in close contact with a lot of people on the plane and in the airports of the trip. I couldn't imagine we were going to be right next door and not see each other. It sounded like the adults were already planning festivities with champagne, which as far as I knew couldn't be drunk through a mask.

We got rid of our travel clothes and put on shorts, tank tops, and flip-flops. "What about masks?" I asked. "They weren't wearing any."

"Put one in your pocket, and let's play it by ear," said Papi.

Dad stood in front of the mirror and looked at his tank top. And then, in what seemed to be his vacation habit, peeled off the tank top and changed into a T-shirt. Papi and I looked at him, shaking our heads.

"Come on, Dad," I said.

"Ooh, someone's anxious."

I looked out the window and saw Devlin running up from the water. It had been nearly eight months since we had seen him, and he was definitely more muscular. Maybe I should put on a T-shirt, too, a baggy one to hide the fact that I had wimped out in my workouts over the months. I had tried to make up for it in the last three weeks, doing the morning workouts before I went online for school, but I was sure he was going to comment on my lack of progress.

We all gathered in front of the Saxton's cottage, our family lined up facing their family, but still at a distance. "How should we do this?" said Joanna.

"I'm much too happy to see you to do elbow bumps," said Dad.

Devlin ran over and picked me up in a bear hug. "Good to see you, brother." He got me all wet, and I realized it was my first contact with the Atlantic Ocean. He put me down and squeezed my biceps. "Not bad. Aren't you going to show Livie?"

She stood a few yards away, her hands twisted in front of her as if she was nervous. The moment of truth. We were both fifteen now. My birthday was right before we left, and we had decided to postpone the celebration until we got to the Bahamas. At least for a few weeks, we would be the same age until Olivia turned sixteen in November. Olivia and I had a video chat on my birthday just a few days before, but the first face to face in over ten months made me feel awkward. And a person just looks different in person. Neither a video or camera can begin to capture the live magic of a smile or the tiny little movements of a person's eyes.

When I had first seen her from our porch, her long legs stretched out on the chair, she was wearing a bikini the color of the sky. Now she had a large T-shirt over her suit that said Island Life in pink script. We stared at each other. Someone had to make a move. I took a few steps forward and put my arms around her. I whispered, "I fucking hate it when you leave."

"But we just got here," she giggled. "Nobody's leaving for ten days."

I sighed and hugged her tight. We didn't kiss.

I had meant to monitor how the greeting went between my dads and Devlin, but I was a little distracted and missed it.

"Let's go up on the veranda," said Joanna. "Nigel, be a dear and get the champagne."

There weren't enough chairs, so Devlin, Olivia and I sat on the wooden stairs. Nigel popped the cork and filled five glasses. Olivia and I got ginger beer. We all clinked glasses.

"Wait," said Devlin. "Let me get my phone. I want to get a photo of the toast."

Olivia and I moved to the top step. Devlin stood on the bottom step and stretched out his arm to get us all in a selfie. "Everybody say Swiss cheese." He snapped several pics.

We passed the phone around to look at the pictures.

"Aren't we just a lovely mix of colors?" said Joanna. "Including my pasty white husband."

"I'm working on a proper tan," said Nigel.

Joanna laughed. "More like a proper burn." She began to sing, "We are the world."

"Oh, please, Mum," said Olivia.

"Well, look at us. We have Bahamian, British, Jewish, Mexican, and Colton with his lovely mix of..." she stopped and seemed to realize she had gotten little carried away and didn't know exactly what I was. I hadn't told Olivia about the results of the DNA test and I doubted my dads had told Joanna. I wasn't sure exactly why. Maybe we were all a little embarrassed that Joy had screwed up. I glanced at my dads and they had twisted smiles.

Nigel jumped in. "How is your novel coming along, Augie?"

Dad's face relaxed with the change of subject. "Oh! I sent it to a publisher, and they offered me a contract."

"That's wonderful, Augie," said Joanna. "You didn't tell us."

"There has been so much going on. I only got the email a couple of weeks ago. I'm thrilled."

"What's it about again?" asked Joanna.

I jumped up. "Olivia and I are going for a walk."

"Colton!" said Dad. "How rude. We're talking."

Nigel was surprisingly the one to be sympathetic. "Go on, you two. I'm sure you don't want to hear your parents prattle on."

"Don't go far," said Papi. "We need to think about dinner. I would like to have a decent meal."

"Alone at last!" I said when Olivia and I got a distance away. "If I have to hear Dad talk about his novel one more time, I'm going to scream."

"I think it's brilliant your dad wrote a book," said Olivia.

"He used me. I'm going to ask for part of the royalties."

Olivia let out her sweet laugh I had missed so much, again the in-person version ten times better than the online version. "Is it actually about you?"

"He says it's not. It's inspired by true events, but the story, names and characters are quite different, so he says."

"I suppose you'll have to read it to find out."

"It won't be out for a year."

"By that time, all this mess should be over, and we can take a proper vacation to San Francisco or you to England." She had a moment of hopelessness in her eyes but quickly sent it away with a smile.

We walked to the water and waded in up to our knees. "It's warm," I said. "The water in California is never like this, even in Southern California in the middle of summer."

"You told me you were getting the DNA test, but you never said the results. Mum nearly stuck her foot in it, not knowing to describe you as Black Jewish or Black Mexican."

"I guess I'm Blatino."

"Oh. Ruben is your dad, then?"

We stood in the water, staring out at the gentle waves. The sun was going down, giving everything a rosy light. I so didn't want to talk about this right now. It was supposed to be a magical moment—reunited with my girlfriend in a beautiful, warm place by the ocean and the setting sun. She turned toward me, waiting for an answer. "They're both my dads," I said.

"Of course. But there was the disease thing, and you wanted to know your biological dad."

The problem with being close to someone is that you feel comfortable telling them everything. It had been so easy on phone calls and texting, just blurting out whatever was going on in my life. No filter. But when something comes up in person you'd prefer not to share, it takes on a huge meaning, like I'm lying to her if I hold back. I thought about making up a story that the results got contaminated and we had to do it again. I couldn't lie to her. And what did it matter, anyway. She didn't like me for who my biological father may or may not be. "Here's the deal," I said. "We had a little surprise with the results. Turns out my actual biological father was this Puerto Rican dude who Joy had sex with when she wasn't supposed to and he got killed in Iraq."

"Now that's a pisser. Sorry. I'm a bit gobsmacked. Are you okay?"

"On the bright side, I don't have to worry about that disease and my dads don't have to deal with who won the sperm race. It's just that I'm more of a stray dog than I thought."

"Don't be daft. Your parents are great. Look around you. We're in this wonderful place."

She was right. I was an idiot to think there was anything negative going on. I had an urge to kiss her, but I was sure the parents were watching from the porch.

"Colton," shouted Papi. "Come back. We're going to eat."

Twenty-One

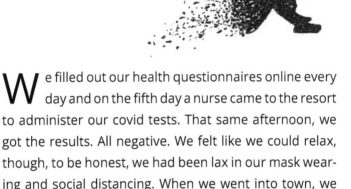

We filled out our health questionnaires online every day and on the fifth day a nurse came to the resort to administer our covid tests. That same afternoon, we got the results. All negative. We felt like we could relax, though, to be honest, we had been lax in our mask wearing and social distancing. When we went into town, we wore masks, but most of the locals did not and stared at us like we had at the mask wearers when we were in Hong Kong.

The adults used the test results as an excuse to break out more champagne. They all sipped their drinks while stretched out on the lounge chairs under colorful umbrellas. Nigel had gotten a terrible sunburn and was peeling. Olivia and I lay on towels on the beach about halfway to the water, but we could still hear their conversation.

"They do go on with their chinwagging," said Olivia. "Maybe they'll all get drunk and pass out, giving us some peace." I laughed and took her hand.

Devlin expressed his frustration with his architecture career being postponed due to the pandemic. "I think I might get about a hundred tattoos and go off and join

Cirque de Soleil."

"He's always been like this," said Joanna. "I'm convinced they switched out my baby at the hospital."

"Of course," said Devlin. "They miraculously found a replacement with Dad's eyes and your exact nose."

"He used to paint his toenails. One day, the headmaster called me in and said he had punched another boy who called him a bender. So, my dear son says, 'Mum, I didn't punch him because he called me gay; it's because he's an arsehole. I've been waiting for an excuse.' I was perfectly ready to defend him for standing up for himself, and then he says a thing like that. Sometimes I'm afraid we've spoiled him terribly."

Devlin laughed. "Bollocks! You never would have flown thousands of miles so I could have a little romance. And with a Yank, no less."

Olivia rose up on one elbow and turned her head to give him a dirty look.

"That's not why we're here, Dev. We're all exhausted with the pandemic and needed a break," said Joanna. "And we're delighted our Yanks could join us and that Olivia can spend some time with Colton. I know you are, too."

Devlin stood up and walked toward the water. In passing by us, he kicked a little sand at Olivia. "Bastard," she mumbled.

Where the sand was more hard-packed, he threw his hands to the ground and did a handstand. He scissor-kicked his legs and walked into the sea on his hands. Olivia turned onto her stomach and faced the parents with her hand on her chin, as if she didn't want to be her brother's audience while he showed off. I mimicked her position.

"When I told Dev what happened to your nephew," said Joanna, "he was surprisingly torn up about it, I mean, for someone he's never met. He always has this happy-go-lucky façade, but he's quite sensitive."

"I wonder where he gets that?" said Nigel.

Joanna laughed. "How is your sister doing, by the way?"

"She's had a tough time. It must be unimaginable for a mother to lose her firstborn."

"You're giving me shivers," said Joanna.

"You brought it up, my dear," said Nigel. "I don't believe I know the details."

"My sister's ex-husband and son were on their way as part of a group called the Proud Boys to counter-demonstrate against a Black Lives Matter march. They had an assault rifle in the truck and Jason attempted to frighten two women in a car with Black Lives Matter and Biden stickers on it. His father was distracted and lost control of the car."

"My God! Have you thought about writing the tragedies of 2020 into a novel? You could call it An American Year of Infamy," said Nigel.

"Thought about it, yes. Not sure I can yet."

Devlin came out of the sea, flicked water on us and shook out his curls as he walked toward the adults. He stood over them and rubbed his abs. "All this eating and lying around. I don't want to get fat like my mum and dad."

Joanna picked up a flip-flop and threw it at him, but he was able to dodge it. He looked at Papi, who lay on his stomach and seemed to be asleep. Devlin put a finger to his lips, crept close to Papi, and plopped face down on top of him. Papi shrieked and Devlin rolled off, laughing hysterically.

"I apologize for my son," said Joanna. "He has zero boundaries despite all our best efforts."

"You ruined my beautiful dream!" said Papi.

"I thought I was your beautiful dream."

Papi stood up. "I'll get you!" He grabbed a handful of sand and threw it at Devlin.

Devlin turned and ran toward the water. "You can't catch me!"

I sat up, so I could watch both Devlin and Papi near the water and the reaction from the others on the porch. I was a little worried that Papi might actually be mad. The drama with my dads and Devlin was getting a little annoying.

Papi was shorter than Devlin, but solid and in good shape for a man in his early forties. He caught up with Devlin just as they got to the water and tackled him. They surfaced and started splashing like teenagers. It didn't look like angry splashing.

Dad looked at Joanna and shrugged.

"I'm so sorry," said Joanna.

"Boys will be boys. Ruben can take care of himself."

"Mum," shouted Olivia. "Can't you do something about Dev? He's making a tit of himself."

Papi and Devlin emerged from the water and started

walking down the beach.

"Oops! I've lost my husband," said Dad.

"No, you've gained a son or a brother or something," said Joanna. "He thinks the world of you two."

"He's quite a unique and wonderful person," said Dad.

"We always hoped he would be a free spirit. Not sure we're actually prepared for what we got."

"Oh, rubbish, Joanna, would you have done anything differently?" said Nigel.

"Probably not. I suppose I should say the world might not be ready for what we got."

"When Colton was born, I was petrified about being a parent, of doing the wrong thing, of being a major screwup."

Dad glanced at me and I gave him a what's-up shrug. "I can hear you, Dad." I don't think he heard me because he just waved.

"Oh, no, Augie. He's so fortunate to have you and Ruben as his parents."

Papi and Devlin reappeared on the horizon, silhouettes in the late afternoon light. The sky was turning all kinds of colors behind them. Papi looked like he was telling a funny story with lots of gestures, and Devlin would stop and face Papi with interest, the perfect audience. A minute later, Devlin took off running and dove into the pink and purple sea, coming up like a dolphin before diving back under.

Olivia sat up, too, and watched her brother and Papi. "Well, isn't that sweet? Dev and Ruben are like best friends now."

I didn't give any sign I had been worried about them. Another thing I hadn't told Olivia about was Papi's blowup when Dev was in San Francisco. "Why shouldn't they be?"

"Ruben is like old enough to be his father." Her voice had that bite to it that sometimes bothered me, but I shook it off.

"Dev is a lot older than me and we're friends."

"Except a lot of the time he acts like he's twelve."

"Oh, come on. He's really fun."

"And I'm not?"

Why was she doing this? In conversations about her brother, there was no way I could win. "Have you listened to Honne?"

"They're okay."

"Their song 'Free Love' is cool."

"It's a bit light. I like Kamal. Chill with unreal vibes."

"I don't know him. Is he British?"

"Born in London. You know all the best things come from London." She laughed.

I put on a southern hick accent. "Heck, I don't got no experience with things over there in old Europe." I was making a joke of it, but I was annoyed she still had that attitude thing about British versus American.

A Frisbee landed at my feet and I looked around to see who had thrown it. Thank you, Dev, for this distraction coming at the right moment. I stood up, picked up the Frisbee, and threw it back to him. I ran toward the water and he threw me a long one. I made a diving catch and landed on the ground.

Olivia got up. "I want to play, too."

We formed a triangle to do a three-way toss. She was really good, her throws accurate and with good distance. We continued throwing the Frisbee as the sun started to drop and the colors in the sky turned deeper shades.

"Let's go take some pics of the sunset," said Devlin.

Everyone gathered on the porch of the Saxton's house to watch the sun go down. The sunset wind rattled the palm fronds and pushed fluffy clouds across the sky. It felt like we were a million miles away from the troubles of the world. My dads held hands. After taking a few photos of the sun going into the water, Devlin sat on the ground, leaning against his mother's legs. Olivia and I sat on the steps. She traced the lines on the palm of my hand and giggled. "I see a long and happy life," she said.

Nigel's nose was still in a book. Joanna turned to him. "How can you see? Put your book down and enjoy the last moments of the sunset, dear."

For a minute, as the sun winked and disappeared, I felt this deep happiness. Everything was cool with my dads and Devlin. Joanna and Nigel were relaxed and didn't seem worried that Olivia and I were going to run away and do something stupid. Olivia stopped examining my palm and pulled the back of my hand to her cheek. She seemed back to enjoying my company, perhaps forget-ting for the moment that I was from across the pond. The wind suddenly died. The silence was like a hum in the air, allowing us to hear in the distance the waves gently hitting the shore. Everything was perfect, giving me a tingling feeling.

We sat there for several minutes without saying anything. I felt like I would remember this moment for a long time to come. But like all perfect moments, something had to break. Nigel swatted his arm with a loud smack, and I think we all jumped a little bit.

"Mosquito?" asked Joanna.

Nigel stood up. "I'll get the repellent."

And then the solar porch lights came on and there was talk of dinner and more champagne and maybe a walk into town after dinner or a movie on Netflix. The world had stopped for a split second and now was turning again.

We had gotten roasted chicken and salad fixings in town earlier. We gathered in the Saxton's house and sat around their big table. After we ate, everyone said they were too lazy for a walk into town, so I got up to scroll through the movie offerings on the TV in the living room. It would be a tough choice, trying to please everyone. A comedy? An action movie? A drama? A British baking show? I sat on the couch, so caught up in my search, I didn't notice that everybody else had gathered behind me. Devlin cleared his throat in an obvious way, and I turned around. Devlin was holding a cake with fifteen lit candles. It was a total surprise because my actual birthday had been a couple of days before we left, and they had kept the cake a secret. My dads had said we would celebrate my birthday in The Bahamas, but I assumed they had forgotten. They sang an off-key "Happy Birthday" and set the cake on the coffee table in front of me. I felt emotional, but there was no way I was going to cry with Olivia next to me. I made a wish and blew out the candles. Joanna served the cake and Dad poured a tiny bit of champagne in glasses for Olivia and me for a toast.

I took a sip and made a face. "This is going to ruin the taste of the cake."

"I like the bubbles," said Olivia.

They gave me a few gifts: a shirt in the island batik style with fish imprinted on it from my dads, a paddleball game from the Saxton's, and a large shiny conch shell from Olivia, the kind you would buy from a market but never find on a beach. She held it up to my ear. "You can hear the ocean." It was one of the best birthdays ever.

We all crammed into the small living room to watch the movie I had picked out. Olivia, Devlin, and I sat on the floor while the four parents squeezed onto the couch. Olivia and I laughed a lot, but the others only chuckled a few times and groaned a lot more. Nigel and Dad fell asleep. Dad started snoring.

When it was time to go, the Saxtons walked us out. My dads started toward our place, and I said I'd be there in a minute. Joanna, Nigel, and Devlin went back inside while Olivia and I sat on the steps again.

"Don't stay up too late," said Dad. "We have that tour around the island tomorrow."

We sat quietly for a minute and the motion-sensor porch light went off with a click.

"It was a nice day," said Olivia.

"The best!" I said. "Seriously, having everybody together like that was so great I never want to leave." I probably shouldn't have said the 'leave' word. She gave me a funny look, though it was hard to see her exact expression in the dark.

She yawned. "I'm going inside."

"Did I say something wrong?"

"No. Not at all. I'm just tired." She kissed me on the mouth and said, "Happy birthday," but there was nothing passionate about the kiss. She got up and went in the door.

I walked a short distance toward the water and threw my head back to gaze at the stars. Olivia had left me with a peculiar feeling. She was probably just in one of her moods.

The next day on the van tour of the island, Olivia was quiet and stared out the window a lot. She didn't perk up when we got to a blue hole where we jumped off a platform into a warm inland lake or when we went to the batik factory where we got a demonstration of the process for making the fabric the island was famous for or when her dad bought her a blue dress at the batik boutique. When we got back, I unwrapped my new paddleball set, and Devlin and I played down by the water.

"Is Olivia okay?" I asked him.

"She's just a bit moody sometimes. Nothing to worry about."

I had gotten used to that, but this felt different.

After dinner, I asked her to go for a walk. She hesitated as if she was trying to think of an excuse, but in the end agreed to go with me.

The moon played on the waves and a breeze ruffled the birthday shirt I had put on. I tried to take her hand, but she pulled away. In this most romantic place, I felt romance slipping away. I kind of laughed inside because I didn't really know what romance was and had no experience.

"Is everything okay?" I asked her.

"No worries. Another day in paradise." There was a tiny bit of sarcasm in her voice.

"What happens when we're not in paradise?"

"Exactly."

"Exactly what?"

"Wait for a year to see each other again?"

"It's the pandemic and stuff. It won't always be this way."

"You're forgetting the important fact that we live on opposite sides of the world."

"But...are you breaking up with me?"

"We never actually said we were boyfriend and girlfriend."

"We didn't have to. We felt it, or, at least, I did."

"I'm sorry."

"Wait. That's it?"

"We should go back."

"I need some kind of explanation," I said desperately.

She sighed. "We're from different worlds. Next month I'll be sixteen. If a bloke asks me to go out, am I supposed to say no? That I have a boyfriend on the other side of the world that I never see? We have to be realistic. Sorry."

"Why do the British say sorry so much?"

"There you go," she said. "We're different."

The conversation wasn't going anywhere. If I kept asking her why, it sounded whiney, and I wasn't likely to get an answer I would be pleased with.

We walked back in silence. I left her at her door and headed to our bungalow. My dads were sitting on the porch. As I walked up the steps, the porch light came on, and it felt like a spotlight in my face. I was hoping to sneak in and go to my room. "That was a short walk," said Papi.

"Was it?"

"Everything okay?"

"Sure." I was sad and confused. But more than that I was embarrassed that I had built this fantasy that wasn't real, embarrassed that I wasn't good enough for her because I was the child of a surrogate mom and an unknown father and she had two nice, normal parents and was British and beautiful.

I tried to walk by them, but Dad reached out and touched my arm. "Things always look different in the morning." He hadn't been fooled for a second that everything was okay. "Goodnight, son."

"Goodnight... uh... Dads." I couldn't believe I hesitated on the dad part and the way I said it sounded bitter rather than warm. It left a burning feeling in the pit of my stomach. I rushed into the house and into my room. I collapsed on the bed, feeling small, worthless, and undeserving of love. I kicked off my shoes and crawled into bed with the sound of the surf hitting the beach and reminding me of the beautiful place I was in. It was not a reminder I wanted and only made me feel worse. I put the pillow over my head, blocking out sound and light.

Things did look different in the morning, not a whole

lot better, but not the catastrophe it seemed the night before. The worst thing was how I had treated my dads. It was a moment's hesitation. I wasn't even sure they had noticed. But inside me it felt like I had slapped them both across the face, hesitating a second to call them my dads. Why did they put up with me? Maybe the Puerto Rican guy was a bad person, and I had inherited his nature.

I walked into the kitchen in the morning with the heaviness I had aged years. Dad was at the table on his laptop and Papi was making breakfast. They both stopped and looked up. I felt as bad as I had ever felt. "I'm such a disappointment," I said. My words were shaky, and tears welled up in my eyes.

Dad jumped up, and they both came around the table to me and pulled me into a hug.

"You are the exact opposite of a disappointment," said Dad.

"You are our life," said Papi.

How many times in my life had a mere touch or word from them eased my pain? I melted in their arms and they let me cry. I didn't have to tell them what happened with Olivia. They knew. No matter what happened in my life, I had the absolute certainty they would always be there for me and love me, even in those times when maybe I didn't deserve it. The next few days would be difficult, but I knew Devlin would throw his arms around my shoulders and be my big brother. Joanna would be more of a surrogate mom to me than the one who carried me for nine months. But Olivia would be nearby and a constant reminder of the person I had become so dependent on in the last year, someone just for me, someone I could tell all my stuff to, but lost. She had a couple of days to change her mind, but I knew she wouldn't because her words had been so sure. For the second time on a trip outside the country, I would be going home to uncertainty. This time it was online school indefinitely, no basketball practice, limited contact with friends, and no calls and texts from across the ocean to look forward to.

I picked up my phone and looked at my messages. Elijah had texted saying I must be having a good time because he hadn't heard from me. "Pinchy CAB-ron!" He also said he had some new recipes he wanted me to try, and his mom was doing better. She was back to chatting online with the Mexican guy. Fer had sent a message that things were boring without me around and he hoped everything was going well with Olivia. He also mentioned he had run into Josh and he had asked about me. Lio had sent a picture of him and Lettie with their arms around each other at Lake Merritt. He said she had some ideas about a new hairstyle she thought would look good on me.

I had a hundred things running through my head all at once, but Papi brought me back to earth. "How would you like your eggs, mijo?"

"Let me make them," I said. "I have an idea."

"That's the spirit," said Dad. "Like a phoenix rising from the ashes."

"Whatever you say, Dad. Do we have any cheese left?"

Acknowledgements

First, I would like to thank the team at Spectrum Books for inviting me into the family and bringing this book to fruition. They have been supportive of and sympathetic to my vision in this book.

I definitely need to tip my hat to Bevan Vinton for encouraging me to continue the story of the four Burd siblings from Four Calling Burds into First Born Sons, and now this book. Bevan also proofread the manuscript, providing another set of eyes and suggestions to my words.

I have never shied away from writing characters who are diverse in terms of ethnicity, race, gender, and sexual orientation, but I haven't been able to do that without a lot of help. I particularly needed assistance with the character, M, who goes through FTM transition in First Born Sons and reappears in this book as Colton's uncle. Kalil Cohen provided the perspective of a trans man and offered a number of suggestions for the character M.

I have also been very fortunate to have many Black and Latinx friends and family members in my life. My intention has never been to interpret their experiences, but rather to include Black and Latinx stories so vital to the fabric of our society. I thank my husband, Robert Green, and our family for enriching my life and helping me tell those stories, including Divij Anderson-Santibañez, Sharon Anderson, Francisco Santibañez, Dorothy Green, Saundra Green, Stefan Nixon, and Shaun Nixon.

My siblings, Bill Meis, Michael Meis, Mary Hardcastle, Monica Wellman, and Marcia Meis have not only been supportive, but have also showed me all the ways that siblings can have distinctive and nourishing relation-ships.

Floyd Rocker offered help with the dialogue of the British characters and Joan Rosenberg has shared her expertise in marketing. I'd also like to shout out to my Instagram wizard, Natasha, for her marketing expertise. I'd also like to acknowledge some of my readers who have been par-ticularly loyal in offering help and suggestions: Francisco Trujillo, Erin Scholnick-Lee, David Jackson Ambrose, Mar-vin Neu, Richard May, Wayne Goodman, Gilberto Leon, John Hamill, Jose Caratini, James Janko, Jerry L. Wheeler, Jose Rivera, Louis Flint Ceci, Morgan Meis, Stefany Anne Golberg, Lena Taylor, Marika Meis, and Paul Skender.

And finally, I thank the members of the Bay Area Queer Writers Association (BAQWA) for their support.

About the Author

Vincent Traughber Meis grew up in Decatur, Illinois where he got his start writing plays for his younger sisters to act in for a neighborhood audience.

He graduated from Tulane University in New Orleans and worked for many years as an English as a Second Language (ESL) teacher in the San Francisco Bay Area, Spain, Saudi Arabia and Mexico, publishing many academic articles in his field. As result of his extensive travels and time abroad he published a number of pieces, mostly travel articles, but also a few poems and book reviews, in publications such as, *The Advocate*, *LA Weekly*, *In Style*, and *Our World* in the 1980's and 90's.

He finally arrived at his true writing love: novels and short stories. Five of his six published novels are set at least partially in foreign countries and his book of short stories focuses on countries around the world. Several of his novels have won Rainbow Awards, and his most recent novel, *The Mayor of Oak Street* was awarded a Reader Views Silver Award. He has published short stories in a number of collections and has achieved Finalist status in a few short fiction contests. When he's not writing, he works in the garden and travels with his husband. He lives in San Leandro, California.

Excellent LGBTQ+ fiction by unique, wonderful authors.

Thrillers Mystery Romance Young Adult & More

Join our mailing list here for news, offers and free books

Visit our website for more Spectrum Books www.spectrum-books.com

Or find us on Instagram @spectrumbookpublisher

Made in the USA
Columbia, SC
19 February 2023

12530753R00143